THE TROUBLE WITH LANGUAGE

REBECCA
FISHOW

TRNSFR BOOKS *Grand Rapids, MI*

THE TROUBLE WITH LANGUAGE

STORIES

Published by Trnsfr Books
Grand Rapids, Michigan
trnsfrbooks.com

This is a work of fiction. Names, characters, businesses, places, and incidents are the product of the author's imagination or are used fictitiously. Any resemblance to actual events, locales, or persons, living or dead, is purely coincidental.

Library of Congress Control Number: 2020943900
ISBN 978-1-7355727-0-3 (hardcover)
ISBN 978-1-7355727-1-0 (e-book)

Book design by Alban Fischer
Printed in the United States of America
Distributed by Small Press Distribution: spdbooks.org

Trnsfr Books 006
First Edition

For Daniel

CONTENTS

I

None of This Is Your Fault / 3

Timothy's Severed Head / 5

Strangers / 27

Fifteen Days and Fifteen Nights / 29

Mistaken About the Whole Thing / 31

Visiting Sarah, 2005 / 33

Something to Do, Someone to Love / 47

II

Jailbreak / 65

Unlike Any Other Day / 71

The Last Day of School / 74

The Cyclops Has His Reasons / 77

Two Dogs / 80

Brockville, 1972 / 82

The Tall, Thin Man / 95

Everything Was Quicksand / 97
An Exercise in Etiquette / 99

III
The Trouble with Language / 133
Rapid Shrinking / 135
Getting Out of This House / 137
Outside and Inside / 139
Yes and No / 141
A Failed Kidnapping / 145
The Opposite of Entropy / 153
Going to the Diner / 155
Armies / 157
I Too Am Only Dreaming / 159
The Day There Was a Picnic / 165
Ipseity Epistolary / 167
What We Bury / 172
Three Women I Almost Loved / 174

Acknowledgments / 179
Publication Credits / 180

Who hasn't asked himself, am I a monster or is this what it means to be human?

CLARICE LISPECTOR

NONE OF THIS IS YOUR FAULT

Last Sunday I nearly ran over your dog. I couldn't have done it without you. Why wasn't he secured in the yard? Why wasn't he tethered by some kind of leash, to some kind of tree?

I admit I had been looking down at the time, rummaging for something below the passenger seat, for a map, a lost love letter, my own severed hand. It seems I am always looking down. On the good days, I am rummaging too.

Last Sunday was not a good day, despite the rummaging. I do not know if life is precious. I do not know who gets to choose what lives and what dies.

Your dog lived, another dog died. Later that day I came out of my apartment and, because I had been looking down, I saw it lying on the empty patio of a French restaurant. He was still, save for the slightest tide of his fleeting breath. His eyes were open. They had become two landing strips for flies. Underneath his tail, a small

3

brown splotch. A wet spot on the concrete around his body widened. I called my lover, who rushed home to help. But he could not help the dog and he could not help me. I could not help him. Funny how we felt like help was what we needed.

I am not doing a lot of living these days. Living requires a name. I've misplaced mine somewhere. I'm still searching though, beneath the passenger seat, where I could not find my severed hand. None of this is your fault. Nonetheless, I implore you, please be more careful.

TIMOTHY'S SEVERED HEAD

I. WHO GETS THE SEVERED HEAD
AND WHAT IT LOOKS LIKE

Whoever's suffered the most receives the severed head. We agree degrees of suffering are subjective, so it's unfair. Still, we're not surprised when the package shows for Timothy. When the doorbell rings, he goes outside and finds it, sits on the stoop, puts his chin in his hands, package beside him like a pet. The sun changes position in the sky.

We arrive at the apartment from our jobs at different hours. Me, my girlfriend Eunice, and Timothy's ex, Mary, join Timothy on the stoop, semicircle him and the boxed severed head. We sit and put our chins in our hands too. We try to imagine what the severed head looks like, but our ideas are fuzzy, imprecise. In our mind, it looks like our own heads, but dead and bodiless.

Mary puts a hand on Timothy's shoulder, says,

"Don't leave us all hanging," so Timothy takes his key, tracks along the center of the packing tape. As he reaches in to unload the severed head, we hope Timothy will feel some relief. We hope the gravity of the severed head will help ease the weight of all his suffering.

Timothy fists its hair and pulls it out, holds the severed head close to his own face like he's holding the head of a lover, tender and immense. We feel weird watching such an intimate moment, so we go inside. Mary spies through the blinds and we join her, watch what Timothy's hands do to the severed head. Mary sighs, looks a little sad and leaves Eunice and me with our good view. We were right. It looks like a version of us, but dead and bodiless.

II. WHAT WE WOULD DO WITH
THE SEVERED HEAD

Timothy will do the right thing with the severed head, eventually. For now, he wedges it snugly between his old boots and the box of childhood toys on the floor of his messy closet. It is Timothy's right to manage the head how he will, nightly take it out, let his suffering speak to it in a ravaged tongue only they share. He collects the severed head's fallen hairs, twists them around his index finger. He presses his thumbs to the eyelids and pulls them down, but when he releases, they spring up and show two whitewashed eyes. Sometimes I hear Timothy whispering, whimpering. Sometimes I hear him laugh.

As much as we want to know more about the severed head, as roommates and friends we respect Timothy's privacy, laze around the living room while Timothy has his head time. I sit on the love seat, Eunice cuddled close. Mary's on the floor making her cat bat a piece of string. We go around and say what we might do, had the severed head come for us instead.

Eunice: take a photograph of the head and Photoshop it onto different bodies. The bodies of celebrities: man-headed Taylor Swifts and Kim Kardashians. The bodies of animals: man-headed whales, caribou. The man-headed body of a baby like ours, our baby who never got born. Eunice would make an army of hybrid bodies that would protect her from pain. Print them, tape them to the walls. Her own suffering would go away, then. It would be trapped inside an army of repurposed heads.

Mary: take care of the severed head, like a husband. Wake it up in the morning, brush its teeth. Bathe it. Make it coffee, fry it eggs, and butter toast. Comb its hair, pack its briefcase. Pin a tie to its neck hole. Summarize the morning news for the severed head, and tell a joke. Wonder what the severed head is thinking.

He's so quiet these days. Wonder if the severed head is growing bored. Wonder if she has sacrificed her dreams so the severed head could achieve its own. Wonder if this life with the severed head will be worth it in the end. But she loves the severed head. It needs her.

Kiss the severed head on the cheek. Find its car keys, winter hat. Wave goodbye to the severed head from the doorway. Fold last night's laundry, return it to drawers. Think about taking up karate, getting some excitement in her life. Wait for the severed head to call during its lunch break, chin in hands. Shower, then put back on her makeup. When the severed head comes home, say, "How was your day?"

See how tired the severed head is? See how little it eats? Give it two Ibuprofen and two Tums. How heavily it hits the pillow. How soundlessly it sleeps? Sleep next to it, but imagine a different severed head lying next to her. Imagine holding its nonexistent hand.

Me: do not tell what I would do with the severed head. Can't explain it. Can't explain what I do with my suffering either. Truth told, I'm not sure I would do the right thing. I'm not sure I do the right thing with my suffering now.

Eunice looks at me like: Toby, that's not fair. We all told, why can't you? But we're high school sweethearts, so she loves me too much to be angry with my silence long. She settles her head back on my chest.

III. HOW THE SEVERED HEAD
CHANGES TIMOTHY

Wakes up earlier.

Listens to experimental jazz in the shower.

Replaces unprescribed Klonopin and Adderall and alcohol with cigarettes.

Loses ten pounds.

Looks better.

Replaces the cigarettes with coffee.

Runs twice a week.

Buys a pair of running pants.

The tight kind that show his junk.

Eats when he's hungry, stops when he's full.

Loses two more pounds.

Donates small amounts of money (a dollar each) to good causes.

The animal shelter. Public radio.

Smiles more.

Fixes the shifters on his bike, oils the chain.

Makes plans to pedal to Portland, just for fun.

Remembers liking Portland as a kid.

We don't know if he'll actually do it. That's
a long-ass way.
Drives his box of childhood toys to the Salvation Army.
Only after asking if we want any.
I want the Matchbox cars. Don't know why.
Hums or sings throughout the day.
Opens the blinds in the apartment.
Comes into our rooms to open our blinds without
asking, just assuming it's what we want.
It's annoying, but we're happy he's feeling
better.
We close them when he leaves.
Buys a plant.
Asks Mary to teach him how to care for it.
Sometimes feeds Mary's cat for her.
I bet he's taking good care of the head, too.
Brushing its hair, spraying it down.
Makeup?
Visits the grave of his mother, Dawn, and his grand-
mother's grave.
They were both suicides.
His mother had schizophrenia,
was a sometimes-prostitute.
A meth addict.
I don't know anything about his
grandmother.

Visits his older brother, Jeff.

In prison.

He'll be out and at the halfway house soon.

Applies for a managerial position in the Shop N' Save fish department.

Gets the job.

Tells us he's been thinking a lot about suffering.

Necessary vs. unnecessary suffering.

When he gets overwhelmed or anxious, thinks about death.

Not in a morbid way, in a way that calms.

Like, one day, he will be dead.

And then what will any of this suffering matter?

So what should it really matter now?

IV. WHERE THE SEVERED HEAD CAME FROM

[TIMOTHY *and* TOBY *talk while eating breakfast in the kitchen. The severed head is propped up on its own seat.*]

TOBY: It's weird that the severed head can help a person.

Like, it's pobably more useful now as a head than it could have been as a complete head-and-body.

TIMOTHY: A part worth more than the sum of all parts.

[*Pause.*]

Where would you guess it came from?

TOBY: Sometimes I think it just materialized. Never had a body in the first place. It's from another dimension where all the people are just severed heads floating, or like swimming around. Yours is one of the dead ones. It wrote in its will that, after it dies, it wants to be sent to a sufferer in our dimension.

TIMOTHY: I like that.

TOBY: Like it donated itself to faith.

TIMOTHY: That's close.

TOBY: Or maybe it's the head of some journalist who terrorists decapitated in the Middle East. Or it came from a prisoner of war.

TIMOTHY: If you look really close, it has tiny wings sprouting in back near the neck hole. I thought the flaps were just the skin peeling off, but it's an angel. One of those head cherubs, only a deformed one.

TOBY: A dead cherub. A stillborn?

[TIMOTHY *rises, walks, put his bowl in the pile of dirty dishes, and picks up the head.*]

TIMOTHY: Still an angel, though. Still my angel.

[TIMOTHY *exits.* TOBY *sits alone.*]

TOBY: Maybe Eunice is my angel.

Saturday, about ten in the morning, awake in bed. Our bed's a mattress on the floor. Eunice keeps saying she wants to get a box spring, a frame. Join the land of adults like it's such a good land where everyone's happy.

"And anyways," she keeps saying, "it hurts my back. I have all these lumps."

When I feel her back there may be lumps, but I don't say. My back hurts too, a manageable hurt you get used to.

Eunice has practice on Saturdays, so I'm in bed alone, scribbling out my play script. In high school, I was voted class writer, and Eunice won class dancer. I wrote three one-act plays that the drama club performed. She would dance every day after school. Ballet, hip hop, you name it. She's got long legs, a dancer's body, banging in a leotard and tights. She's also a really good dancer, pop-star-backup-dancer good.

When we got pregnant we decided not to keep it. Then, her parents kicked her out and cut her off. Now she only dances on Saturdays with some girls, pitches in to pay a guy for an unheated practice room. They've done one show at the mall, another at a nursing home. She says those make her depressed because she sees her future. One day, she'll dance on real stages, and we'll have a kid for real.

I look at the ceiling crack, roll, look at the dust bunnies, the cobwebs in the corner. Timothy's closet is on the other side of the wall. It's possible the severed head's staring straight at me, sending me good vibes. "Hey, head," I say, and wonder if he's named it. "I hope you're enjoying your stay."

I put down my pad of paper. Downstairs, I hear Mary making coffee in the kitchen, and getting going the Easy Mac she eats each morning. Mary's gone distant in the past few days, only really talks to Eunice. I hear the front door open, and Eunice dropping her gym bag. They start talking, so I get out of bed, change my boxers.

Downstairs, Eunice's got that glow, a mix of sweat and gentle euphoria like she's spent two hours in a forgetful trance where the real world doesn't factor. She's wearing her leotard, sitting at the table, straddling a backwards chair. Mary's in pajamas perched on the counter, looking like she hasn't slept in days. When they see me they shut up.

"Hi," Eunice says, and spoons herself some noodles.

"Morning," I say, kiss her on the cheek. "Any more of that Easy Mac for me?"

Eunice says I can have a bite of hers, holds her bowl out, but frowns like she doesn't really want to share. I probe the fridge for whatever else, stop before I find it.

Then there's a sound like someone's failing at working

the front door lock. Footsteps, shuffling, metallic scratching. After a moment, things go silent. Two shadows scroll across the window blinds. Mary gets squirrelly, flashes out of the room.

Someone knocks on the back door, and I don't know why I answer. Two guys in beanies barge in. One bounces my head off the wall so hard I kiss the linoleum floor, pass out for a second but come to. One of the guys slides past us, out the kitchen, up the stairs. Eunice starts screaming like a foghorn in our ears.

"Stop screaming," the guy who stays says. He pushes Eunice to the counter, throws a hand over her mouth, holds his other in his pocket like he's packing. From my spot on the floor, this guy looks familiar: sad green eyes, brown beard. Crinkly skin that looks older than the person it's on.

"Listen," I say. "We don't have a severed head. None of us are that lucky. Clearly."

"Shut the fuck up," he says, and I ask, "Jeff?"

His voice has me years back, to the night before Timothy found his mother, Dawn, dead. I am sleeping over at his house, reading fishing magazines, top bunk, with Timothy. His brother Jeff's on the bottom playing *Final Fantasy VII*. It's late night by the time we startle, smell smoke coming in through the window. We hear Dawn call for us, ask us to join them in the backyard.

Outside, she's alone but waltzing as though hand-in-hand, swaying, laying her head against an invisible someone's chest, acting as though she's being twirled. She dances around a kitchen chair. It's lit ablaze and burning to the grass.

"We have company," she says, and nods towards the someone we can't see. "This is Prince Edward. Say hello, boys."

Jeff looks at us like "play along," so we squeak out greetings to Prince Edward. Then Dawn takes Jeff's hands, commands him to dance, spins him around like a toy boy until she stops abruptly. She freezes, frowns, lets out a laugh. Then her face goes catatonic and Timothy starts to cry.

Upstairs, a gun fires. The second guy runs back to the kitchen. Mary's in the doorway pointing her gun at him.

"Get out!" Mary yells, and away the robbers go.

"It stinks up there," she says.

VI. REASONS A THIEF MIGHT WANT THE SEVERED HEAD

Sell it on the black market to some dealer who will sell it to some museum.

The severed head deserves museum status, anyways.

Use the money to:

     Pay rent.

     Buy a car.

     Buy drugs.

     Buy sex.

     Buy an actual gun.

They are trying to write a play, and desperately need inspiration.

Pack it in a box, send it to a family in Syria, Sudan.

     We're the ones who need the severed head?

          C'mon.

Upside down: a planter.

     Good nutrients.

Give the head: a gift to a suffering loved one.

     A dying mother, unable to feed herself or go to the bathroom alone. Her body so thin that her bones ache whenever she's touched.

          "Leave me alone," the mother growls.

               She used to be so sweet.

     A brother with PTSD.

          Show him he's still alive.

Eat the brains.

     World Anthropology Magazine: some tribal peoples consume the brains of their spiritual leaders to transfer their wisdom.

Get high.

Kick the severed head around a parking lot.

Then just trash it.

Keep it.

Protect and preserve.

Love the severed head.

Absorb its love.

The thief has suffered too long, too deeply.

He needs some relief.

Just

please.

VII. TIMOTHY REFLECTS ON THE SEVERED HEAD

[TIMOTHY *sits at the foot of his bed, looking forward.* RESPECTFUL, AFFECTIONATE, EMPATHETIC, AMBITIOUS, FAMILY-ORIENTED, INTELLECTUALLY CHALLENGING, KINDHEARTED, CONFIDENT, HUMBLE WOMAN *sleeps on one side of his bed. She wears a nose clip and is breathing audibly through her mouth.*]

TIMOTHY: When things go to shit, it's easy to get sucked into this abyss, this pit, and you think, how'm I ever going to get out of this? There's just—

[*Pause.*]

Nothing else.

[TIMOTHY *stands.*]

I have this memory, me and Mary on the first true-warm spring day. We were walking in the park, and I was trying so hard to pretend. She was telling me about something she learned in class, or heard on the radio. I don't remember the exacts because I couldn't pay attention. I kept thinking: How can she find anything interesting enough to waste energy telling it to me? We sat on a grassy hill. She was smiling, happy. People kept jogging by with their dogs, their baby strollers. People chatting in groups, throwing Frisbees. I thought: Why are they doing any of it? My mother committed suicide. I will one day, too. I feel it. Some nights, I lay in bed and imagined myself hanging. Hung either from a rope tied around the bar in my closet or from any random tree in any woods. I never imagined suicide by gun or a mess of pills. I just liked the idea of swaying, my head separated from my body by something thick and solid.

[*Pause.*]

What has the severed head shown me? Do you know how important people are? How good. How they matter, even after they are dead. What Mary and the others did to protect the head. There's so much good in people, and in me too. I want to make it grow.

[TIMOTHY *walks to a mirror hanging on his bedroom wall, talks to his reflection.*]

The severed head is changing. Its colors have shifted from pinkish to ashen. The blood is almost fully drained. I haven't had to sop up a blood puddle in two days.

[TIMOTHY *assesses his face and body, tries out various poses and facial expressions.*]

Its eyes've gone cloudy translucent, two puddles of oil. I tried to brush its hair the other day, but it came out worse than a shedding dog.

[TIMOTHY *runs his hand through his hair, winks at himself, sniffs the air, puts on a nose clip.*]

It smells warm in here, and rotting, like the earth.

[*As* TIMOTHY *undresses,* MARY *pokes her head in from a door stage left, as if to enter the bedroom, but she stops herself and watches from the doorway, unnoticed.* TIMOTHY *runs a hand down his chest, lifts an arm, and flexes. He goes to the bed and reaches under the covers. He runs his hands over* RESPECTFUL, AFFECTIONATE, EMPATHETIC, AMBITIOUS, FAMILY-ORIENTED, INTELLECTUALLY CHALLENGING, KINDHEARTED, CONFIDENT, HUMBLE WOMAN's *body.*]

I know what's going to happen in the end.

[RESPECTFUL, AFFECTIONATE, EMPATHETIC, AMBITIOUS, FAMILY-ORIENTED, INTELLECTU- ALLY CHALLENGING, KINDHEARTED, CONFI- DENT, HUMBLE WOMAN moans.]
Let me love you.

VIII. THINGS THAT REMIND US OF THE SEVERED HEAD

Toby: Eunice. I tell her, "You're my severed head." The first time I said it she kissed me, called me sweet. Now she just looks a little sad and says, "Yup."

Mary: When she was a kid, there was this really bad car accident by her house. Some guy's body lay out on the pavement, with just a smashed slit at end of his neck. No head. The cops searched and searched the woods by the road for the head, even brought the dogs. Now she keeps wondering about that guy from the car accident. Did they ever find the head? Did they bury him without it? The service couldn't have been open casket.

Sometimes she pictures the unstable, stumbling body scouring the earth for his severed head.

Eunice: It's not so much what reminds her of the severed head, but what the severed head reminds her.

IX. FOR EVERY ACTION THERE IS AN EQUAL AND OPPOSITE REACTION, EVEN WHEN IT COMES TO SEVERED HEADS

By now, we're wearing nose clips most of the time inside. I'm on the porch where the air's good. Mary's in the living room, sulking on the couch. She hasn't gone out in three days, and silences the phone when her work calls. She torpedoes her hand into a chip bag, looks like she's packed on Timothy's shed pounds.

When Eunice comes in the room, asks Mary to talk to her, she doesn't see me through the tilted blinds. The window's up, so I take out my earbuds, try to get some insight into Eunice's recent withdrawal.

"What's up?" Mary asks.

"I'm moving out at the end of the month," Eunice says.

Mary sits straight. "Really?"

"This is my only life. All this nothing I've been doing, and it's going to be over soon. Like, I don't want to waste my only life anymore." She stands, starts pacing the room like an animal stuck in a circus train cage.

"What about Toby?" Mary asks.

"He wants a baby I don't want with him. He still thinks he's a playwright."

I get up, sit down, get back up, pace the porch. I contemplate yelling, "What is this, Eunice!" but can't bring myself to speak.

"I was there for all of Timothy's shit," Mary says. "His depression. His suicide shit. I'm the one who pulled the gun on Jeff last week."

"He's really changed," Eunice says.

"He's gotten better and forgot me."

"I'm not saying I'd do him or marry him or anything, but I would definitely do a guy like Timothy. His new girlfriend's really hot."

"It's like everything I did for him doesn't even count."

"You should leave too," Eunice suggests.

My vision tunnels and I feel queasy sick. I think to just start walking down the road, cool off, but Timothy pulls up the drive.

"Hey buddy," he says, and gets out of his car.

He swings a clear bag full of some kind of meat, unties it, pulls out a fish.

"Dinner," he says, smiling like a fool. "Chopped the heads off myself."

🕊

X. WHAT TIMOTHY DOESN'T DO WITH
THE SEVERED HEAD

Offer it to Mary as a gift for loving him so well.

Like an engagement ring, but more sincere.

Taxidermy and mount it.

Keep it forever.

It came for him. Why not?

Give it to Jeff.

Degrees of suffering are subjective, but Jeff's right up there with Timothy, for sure.

At any rate, it might prevent a second burglary.

Donate it to an art school.

The medical illustration majors can draw it.

Eat the brains.

World Anthropology Magazine: some tribal peoples consume the brains of their spiritual

leaders to transfer their wisdom.

Give it to me.

I'm lost.

Play god.

Leave it in the park so a stranger can find it.

Put it in a box with a stamp.

Send it to a stranger.

Turn their life around.

Twist it onto a stake.

Stick said stake in the front yard.

Let everyone get a look.

Take out an ad in the local newspaper.

Found: severed head.

Brown hair, green eyes, about ten pounds.

Useful and effective, but looks a little scared.

Rapidly decomposing.

XI. WHAT TIMOTHY DOES WITH
THE SEVERED HEAD

We call the girls, leave voicemails. Email. Timothy goes
so far as to send invitations in the mail. I miss Eunice.
Her long legs, her sad smile. I keep imagining a baby
that has both of our faces. I miss the way she loved me.
Now I don't know who to talk to feel better. If I got the
head, I'd have shown Eunice, made her want to stay. We
might not have the right numbers and addresses. We
hear back nothing.

The sky is elephant gray. It's summer, hot in a comfortable way it hasn't been yet. When the rain slows,
Timothy and I take to the woods behind the apartment.
I carry the spade. He's got the bagged head slung over
his shoulder like a snack. We sweat, peel our sweatshirts
off, walk a little farther.

He says, "Here's good," and his digging's rhythmic. A bird crows a song. I haven't spent this much time in the forest since I was a little kid. It's good, fresh, alive. The rain has amplified all the earthy scents. I like the way the world smells, the air feels, the trees sway.

"Trees don't look anything like us," I say. "Except in some ways they do."

"They have bodies," he says. "They're alive."

When the digging's done, Timothy uncovers the head, places it in the hole. He takes the spade and tosses in some soil.

"I feel like I should make a speech," he says, but doesn't.

We stand around a couple minutes, then we head back home.

STRANGERS

I went down to the old mill building and stood between the river and the massive brick walls. I thought about the hundreds of girls who had once gotten sick there, turning cotton into pieces of the American Dream. I seemed to remember the whole building on fire, the girls leaping to their deaths, like sunny angels choosing one horror over another.

The memories weren't why I came. They never are, and yet I always seem to find them. I had come to sip wine and view the art exhibition hung along the renovated hallways. I wandered through the halls for miles until the art felt like memories, too.

For a breather I snuck into a broom closet. I took a seat between a ladder and a mop, reveled in the cool, dark quiet. Then, a little girl revealed herself from a tall shelf she had been hiding behind. The girl had one normal, girl-sized arm, and another as short and thin as a pine needle. She looked very ragged. She stayed very quiet. "Do you know where you live?" I asked the girl, leading her out of the closet, into the hall. "Maybe we can find your mother." But she did not know where she lived, and she had no mother to remember, so I carried her home.

My lover arrived and I showed him our new child. The girl and I, eating peanut butter sandwiches at the kitchen table. I prepared a bed for her on the couch in the living room, but all night she sat on my lap until we rocked to sleep together.

When I woke, the child was gone. Another woman, full-grown with two full-grown arms, sat on the couch across the room. Ragged clothes and gray, soft teeth. She said she only wandered in to find a little warmth.

"You can stay," I told her, and my lover, too. Because I knew it was going to be like this. Strangers coming in for me to love them, strangers going away.

FIFTEEN DAYS AND
FIFTEEN NIGHTS

I drove my car two days to the ocean because I didn't see the difference between doing that and anything else. Whatever I thought to say to you from the driveway, I could have said anything else. I said I had been sliding around like an olive in an emptied martini glass. You are not the glass. Perhaps you are an olive branch.

There's nothing like the ocean. Its long blanket of self. The way it crashes back and back over the span of almost forever. The way it attaches itself to the moon with invisible threads. It attached itself to me as I maneuvered into its cold bulk. I instructed my body not to feel. I stood in the water for fourteen days, knee-deep.

I watched vacationing families: a young man, his two daughters naming every wave. I listened to builders erect the new face of a bungalow, blurting out measurements. At one-thirty, they climbed down their ladders for

29

lunch. An old man and his oscillating metal detector. A bottle cap, a piece of broken sunglasses. The sun, broken in the clouds. People packing up. Each wave rhymed with all other waves.

At night I counted reflections of stars. Twenty-four. Forty-two? How many stars had already burnt out?

The ocean rolled and roiled.

On the fifteenth morning I fell asleep. I stayed asleep so long that when I woke the ocean was doing the very same thing.

MISTAKEN ABOUT
THE WHOLE THING

For a moment, I truly believed that the war had come home. People ran from the streets. Missiles, directed and released by an invisible enemy, exploded whole city blocks. Trees disintegrated. Angels beyond the clouds finally sang for us.

Families, friends, and total strangers clung to each other with no concern for body odors, bank accounts. Bankers held garbage men. Travel agents held architects. Children climbed into the arms of murderers, and I clung to you. You weren't even there, but we were so close, I couldn't tell whose hair was whose.

If you were here, I hope I would forgive you for starting the war. I hope I would admit that it wasn't all your fault. Together, we could start some kind of peace, fashion a pair of wings out of old curtains and medical dressings. I could repeat the word "gauze" into your ear until it had no meaning. If all went well, we would take turns sewing the wings to our shoulder blades, taking off and coming back. Taking off again.

Today I see I was mistaken about the whole thing. There is no war here, only my one shoe is missing. I had spent so many days taking it off and putting it back on, I don't know what I'll do now.

VISITING SARAH, 2005

You meet me at the San Diego Airport. I am transit-tired, unwashed. I smell my sweat mixing with the thick hibiscus air. You pull up in your pimped-out Altima, its rims shiny, windows tinted opaque as though you are trying to lure people into caring about who is inside. You step out of the car and onto the curb. Skin-tight jeans, sequin tank top, cheap hoop earrings. Fake nails and unnaturally tanned skin, the curls pressed out of your hair. You are done up like a tinsel Christmas tree. It's been two years since I last saw you, before you enlisted in the Marines and I enrolled at the university I cannot afford.

"Yo," you say, and I say, "Yo." Already I am parroting your detached tone. Already I am lying.

"Sup?" you say.

"Not much, sup with you?"

We push my luggage into the trunk and drive. San Diego is palm trees dusting blue skies, a warm breeze, and manicured boulevards. The people here have long legs, wear sunglasses. Their sparkly clothes scatter light like rain. Briefcases and loafers, sports bras and jogging dogs, eight-lane highways, cars moving like armies of ants following chemical cues.

On the highway we don't speak. You push the accelerator to the floor, speed a hundred miles an hour through traffic, weave, jerk, keep changing lanes. I freeze and clutch any handle I can find.

"Fuck! Drive faster!" you scream into the traffic, nearly take out another car's side mirror.

Angry as I ever let myself get, I say, "Can you please slow down?"

"No," you say, and that's the end of that.

The guard at Camp Pendleton's gate checks your identification card. Then we're inside the thick calmness of the base, which could be a nature reserve or a national park, except you are saying, "This is where they test the bombs. That's a shooting range. They train on Humvees out that way. Two of my friends died in accidents there."

"I'm sorry," I say, but you say, "Meh. It's sad but it happens," in the same yo-tone you used when you mentioned over the phone, last June, "I'm getting deployed again. They need more bodies in Iraq."

Your room in the barracks is a messy hoard. Piles of unfolded clothes, rucksacks and combat boots, hair dryers, purses, high-heeled shoes. Fast food wrappers, and old magazines, messy like your bedroom back home used to be. I thought the Marines might have made you neat. A broken chair. A BB gun. A blond synthetic wig. The spare top bunk is piled to the ceiling.

When I ask you why you don't have a roommate, you tell me you used to, but you don't like having one. Female Marines are all sluts. And if you're not a slut, the guys still spread rumors that you are. So fuck them all, you don't care. You're not having sex anymore. Fuck that.

"You're not having sex because people will think you're a slut?"

"I just don't want to. I don't like it. I'm just not."

An hour later, we pull up to Maria's condo. Maria is your only female Marine friend. She lives off-base, in the San Diego suburbs, where identical homes look like big storage units, their beige, rough walls lined with potted begonias. Flowers that look like bloody fists.

You tell me, "Ted and Maria are divorced, but he still lives here. It's a money thing. She's really sad. Just don't talk about it."

Inside, two male Marines sit on the living room couch. They are baby-faced, look about sixteen and sound even younger. They play a first-person shooter game, lean alert into the screen, send gunshot blasts and death shouts through the room. Tiny soldiers burst and fall. I wait for the boys to look up, but they don't, so I stop smiling stupidly at them.

We find Maria in the kitchen, pouring tequila into shot glasses. Maria is Mexican-American, and desperately beautiful. Huge sad eyes and small smiling lips, tanned skin glowing like an angel. But she's skeletally thin, concave where convex should be. She cuts lemons with tree-branch hands, is dressed like a winking pinup girl. Her ass cheeks peek out beneath a frilly mini skirt. Her thin legs end in tall stiletto points. You and Maria dress magazine sexy, and I wish I had changed into one of your outfits, like I used to back when we shared a room.

We drink tequila and talk and laugh. We are incredibly sad and having a good time.

Maria says, "Your sister says you're smart."

I shrug. Her words feel more like accusations than compliments. She frowns, looks me up and down.

"You are," you say, "That's why you go to college."

"I don't know," I say, but it's a lie.

"You're really skinny," Maria says, so I know you've told her that I can't stop throwing up.

I wrap my arms around my waist and reply, "Not really." It's another lie, but I'm not as small as Maria. When she disappears into the bathroom to fix her makeup, I say to you, "She's the thin one."

You say, "She doesn't eat when she's depressed," then Maria returns with eyes trapped in fresh eyeliner fences.

We leave the boys with their simulated shrieks. They do not look up as we cross through the room, they just keep shooting the virtual enemies. We settle into the car and you speed towards Mexico. I force myself to relax. I think, you haven't killed yourself driving yet. Why would it happen while I'm here?

"Do you talk to Mom and Dad much?" you ask.

"Sometimes," I say.

"I can't talk to Mom without screaming."

"At least she doesn't yell anymore. Dad's the one who makes me mad. He never helps out, never listens. That's why Mom was so angry all the time."

"Mom just opens her mouth and I get angry," you say. "I don't know how you can stand her."

"I get angry too. I just don't see the point in arguing. She's just worried about you anyways," I say.

"About me? What about you?"

When I ask you to tell me more about what you do at work, what you do when you're deployed, Maria insists that you aren't allowed. I'm a civilian, and you're in intelligence. But you talk anyways, because I'm your sister. You stare at 3-D maps all day. Dots move around the maps and the dots are people. When a dot crosses a wrong line, you alert the higher-ups, who alert the ground troops, who shoot the dots on sight.

"It's boring," you say. "I want to be infantry. I was trained just like the guys, and I'm a sharp shooter, too. I just want to kill someone. But women aren't allowed."

"They should let you."

"The first time I was in Iraq, I filled out casualty reports and that was just as boring as 3-D maps."

Whose casualty reports? I want to know. Soldiers? Civilians? Who's dying?

We park north of the border in a dark lot full of kids like us. We are all abandoning our cars, looking to forget whatever we can, looking to disappear. We walk across the border, laugh across the border. Crossing's a cinch. We flash our passports at a guard, keep moving. We are swallowed deep into a circus city, heavy, jangling, woozy. Stray dogs and strings of lights. Buzzing neon signs. You and Maria soldier past the restaurants and the clubs, as though you have a plan, but I don't know what you want, or where you want to be.

In all directions, men wearing luchador masks blow

whistles. "Don't let the tequila guys near you," you say. "They take your head and tilt it back, pour liquor down your throat. After that you have to pay."

We turn a corner and enter a club that's so loud I could forget my speech has sound. Strobe lights pulse and the room is crowded with flailing limbs, bodies that merge into a many-tentacled monster. We push our way to the back of the room. A bar girl brings us candy-colored drinks that taste like sugar and nothing. You and Maria climb onto a table, so I join you, and we dance. We are above everyone, can see everywhere, but I don't notice the man in black approaching until he is shouting up to us.

"What?" you ask, and bend toward the man to hear. "He wants us to go upstairs to the VIP lounge. He says we can have free drinks."

Maria shoots you a skeptical glance, but I tell you, "Free drinks!"

"Okay," you tell the man in black, so he leads us through the crowd, and up a flight of stairs. I can't tell where I am or where I'm going, but I'm safe because I'm following.

We end up on a balcony above the wild dancers. The walls are painted black. The weak floor quivers when somebody steps. The balcony is empty except for a couple other girls, standing bored, sipping drinks. They don't dance, so I don't dance. I drink but don't feel the alcohol. Still, it is a comfort to put the liquid inside of me, make it go where I can't reach. We watch the dancers until you say, "This is boring. Let's just leave."

I wonder if you are wishing you are back in Iraq, stationed at one of Uday Hussein's confiscated palaces. Back in one of the stories you've told me, lifting weights in the makeshift gym as a bomb whistles straight through the sky.

A bomb whistling through the sky, and all you can do is listen as your adrenaline spikes, and wait to stay alive or die. When the bomb finally hits somewhere else, not there, someone else, not you, you're still breathing, so you wipe sweat off your brow. You take a moment to regain your composure and your hummingbird heart slows to normal. All you can think is phew, survived another one, then pick up a barbell and go on lifting weights.

As we walk towards the stairs, I am not too drunk to notice the man in black lingering by the wall. His arms are crossed, his face alert. He eyes us as we leave.

"I'm hungry," Maria says. "I'm hungry. I'm so hungry," and I am too but I don't say. The man in black takes her arm as we pass.

"Where are you going?" he asks.

"We're leaving."

"No," he says, "you stay."

"We're hungry," says Maria, and points a finger at her mouth.

He follows us through the club and out the front door. He follows as we navigate the street, weave through crowds. We are laughing, but I don't know why.

"I'm hungry," says Maria.

You say, "Here."

A taqueria with mirrored walls, fluorescent lights. We slide into a booth. The man in black takes a back corner seat. A yawning woman brings menus. Maria orders a plate of tacos and the man in black stands and approaches. He pulls a wad of bills from his shirt pocket.

"You're hungry?" he says. "I pay. I pay."

He slaps three bills on the table, then slips back into his corner.

Maria eats the tacos like she hasn't eaten in days. When she speaks there's mania in her voice. "I was raised in Mexico by my grandmother, and I can't even speak Spanish. I feel bad. I'm a bad Mexican. I'm still hungry. I'm starving."

The man returns to slap more bills on our table when she orders a second plate of tacos.

"Stop ordering tacos," you say, but Maria orders two more.

"Stop ordering tacos," we both insist, but she doesn't stop ordering tacos.

From his corner, the man in black calls, "Hey. I'm going to the bathroom. I'll be back, okay? Don't move!"

Maria isn't finished eating her tacos, but you tell us to start moving. You pull Maria up, and she spits taco onto the table.

The waitress shouts to the man in black, "They're leaving! They're leaving!"

We are running, we are leaving, and I don't look back, laughing, moving quickly towards the street.

"Taxi! Taxi!"

A minivan pulls to the curb and we file in. We are laughing, but I don't know why. We are so distracted by our laughter that we do not notice the young Mexican couple, a man and a woman, who file in after us, crawl into the back.

"Border! Border!" you shout at the driver.

The driver cuts through traffic and I don't look back. I don't look back for the man in black, or a final look at Tijuana. I don't look back and I don't look back. I don't look until we've driven around a corner and down another street, until I hear a rustling.

I look back and see the Mexican couple hugging, touching, kissing each other's eyes. Before I look forward, they are embracing. Thrusting and pulsing, limbs entwined. I can't tell where one body ends and the other begins. Then, un-embraced, the woman is pregnant.

Laboring, pushing, giving birth, in a moment, to a son. She wipes him clean with the fabric of her long floral skirt.

The child cries, and she nurses him as he ages before my eyes. He grows restless, breaks free of his mother's arms, toddles from one side of the car to the other, climbing over his parents' laps, cooing and babbling, then forming real words, saying "frightened," "hungry," "tired." His limbs lengthen, muscles harden and expand. Hairs sprout above his lip and on his chin. He wants to keep moving, but there's no longer room, so his father puts a palm on his shoulder and he calms. The boy's hands fold in his teenage lap.

"Sarah," I say, and you say, "What?"

"There's a family in the taxi, and it's growing."

"What are you talking about?"

"Turn around."

But you cannot turn around and you don't see. You're busy holding Maria's head up by her hair.

"Let us off here," you tell the driver when we reach the lot. You pay him and stumble in the direction of the car, but I wait to watch the family climb out of the van. They are older now, the child an adult, the parents' hair gone gray. They walk off into the early morning until I cannot see them anymore.

The next days are sunny as we drive up and down the Pacific Coast Highway. You drive slowly, now. We roll around the curves, sandwiched between the ocean and cliffs. We spend our afternoons lying on the beach, soaking up sun, barely moving. At night, we watch the sun set over an ocean, and I feel a sense of calm.

On my final evening, we leave the beach to go to a party at the condo of the man you're dating. His name is Tom and you blush when you say you think you love him, and describe his arms, his smile, his eyes. But Tom looks like all the other Marines to me. They are all clean-shaven, thick-bodied, baby-faced, yet worn. At the party, I feel boring, tired. I don't want to talk. You drink Jaeger. You drink vodka. You drink beer.

You sit next to your Marine, curl up to his chest, try to climb onto his lap. It's obvious by Tom's stiffness that he does not love you back, but he's trying his hardest not to hurt you. I think maybe it's because you are no longer having sex, or because sometimes your love can look like desperation.

When I think I've been forgotten, I go to the bathroom to make myself throw up. You find me there and ask if I'm all right.

"Tom heard you puking," you say.

I'm just drunk, I tell you, but it's a lie.

I talk with a Marine named Chris. We sit on a couch

and flirt, but I'm only pretending. I want to know who we're fighting, and he tells me we're preparing for China, Iran.

"We're preparing for everywhere, really," he says.

I shake my head, excuse myself to find you.

"I'm tired. I think we should leave."

"Already?" you say. "We just got here."

You show me to a bedroom at the end of a short hallway where I can lie down. I leave the lights off, feel for the bed, climb in, cover myself with the blankets. I spend an hour awake with my eyes closed, until Chris opens the door. We share the bed. We kiss. We don't talk at all. When he puts his fingers between my legs, I think this is the reason you brought me here. Everybody's lonely here, and starved. I am performing a not-dishonorable duty.

When I wake it's close to four in the morning and Chris is gone from the bed. I'm glad I'll never see him again. You and I are the only guests left. There are deep brown spills on the carpet, cups tipped across tables, dirty counters. You don't want to let go of Tom's arm, but he eases you off him, says goodnight.

"Fuck this fucking night," you yell, in the car.

"Calm down," I say, but you can't calm down.

Back in your barracks, I pull myself up to the top bunk, watch you undress. You fling your body around the room. You are angry and then laughing, manic. You are naked and clutching your stomach like a loaf. You jiggle your own flesh with both hands, and say, "The Marines are gonna make me lose weight."

I think, time moves through us, not the other way around. It goes on living through us until we're all used up. You let go of your stomach and kiss yourself in the mirror. Then you shit in the toilet with the door open.

SOMETHING TO DO,
SOMEONE TO LOVE

The summer Victoria comes home and takes her clothes off for money is another summer she is supposed to be making progress.

"Come home and we will help you get help," her father, Richard, says over the phone. "Where else can you afford to live?"

The idea of moving back feels like the opposite of progress, like putting melted ice cream back in the freezer. But the last time Richard offered her anything without charging interest she probably still had her baby teeth. At any rate, he may have been right about what she can't afford. She packs a suitcase and locks her dormitory room.

Victoria's mother fits clean sheets over her childhood bed. Her old bedroom above the garage is a balance of oppression and time, an in-between time where Victoria is suspended until she makes enough progress.

A pyramid of stuffed animals fills a rocking chair. High school art projects and magazine-cutout collages interrupt the walls. Old journals and cheap wooden jewelry boxes collect dust on a bookshelf. Victoria hasn't worn the clothes in the drawers in years, but she searches through them just to be sure there's nothing left she might want.

Her new favorite posture is lying flat. In bed, the burden of gravity distributes evenly across her body. She lies in bed for hours. Most of the day, she watches the daytime networks, candy plots. Pretty women with perky fake breasts compete for the love of hideous men. They binge eat, binge exercise, binge shop. Doctors slice their faces with doll-sized surgery knives. Victoria watches until the stories become so boring they leave her feeling carved out. She grows fidgety with an excess of potential energy, tries to calm herself by rocking on her side.

She could call a friend or take a walk in the patch of woods behind the private school down the street, a bit of nature she used to wander through for hours at a time. She could join the world, pick up a paintbrush, go for a run like she used to, but now she cannot understand what makes these activities any more meaningful than the television screen.

When she has been back a week, Richard asks, "Have you been looking for work?"

She should be able to earn money quickly. Magna cum laude, internships every summer, scholarships and awards piled up; her sitting-still-and-focusing credentials.

"I just got here. I'm supposed to be concentrating on making progress."

"You're an adult," he says. "You should be able to do more than one thing at a time."

By mid-afternoon, he leaves the house to drive a taxi, a temporary job that seems to have turned Victoria's mother, Debra, into a cartoon witch. She pulls out her wine glass and starts in with her complaining. Richard is not making enough money. He meets lowlifes out there, bums, probably even criminals. He disappears twelve hours, overnight, while she stays home going batty all alone. But now that Victoria is back, Debra has someone else to focus on. She plans dinners and cleans up long neglected messes, dust in corners, streaks on windows, cobwebs hanging low in the stairwells. Wine-drunk before sundown, she calls up the stairs, asks Victoria to join her for girl time.

Victoria puts on the outfit she left on the floor the night before, and trudges downstairs. Debra pours her a glass of wine, takes a big sip from her own, and makes a toast.

"To your accomplishments. I'm so proud of you." She hands Victoria a napkin to place under her glass. "I want to bring you to see the girls at work. I've told them all about your school and your art. They think it's amazing how talented you are. They all tell me I did so good raising you."

Victoria looks at her hands, avoids her mother's glossy eyes. Her mother has never been proud of her, she thinks. She only wants to feel proud of herself. Of course Debra's voice shrinks when she asks, "How are you doing?"

"Fine."

The response seems enough to shut Debra up on the subject.

"I bet your father didn't tell you he lost almost half of our retirement money thinking he could day trade stocks. It'll take us years to recover. I didn't want to be working until I die."

"He's depressed," Victoria finds herself saying, though she isn't sure why she is defending him. "His meds stopped working, remember? If he hated the job so much, he shouldn't have to waste his time."

"Depressed is just another excuse."

Victoria closes her eyes and concentrates on her breaths. She reminds herself that feelings are only chemical impulses, small synaptic snaps that do not have to mean a thing.

"He fucked up. Lied. Now I'm alone. When he's not here I wake up at every sound thinking, is that a burglar? What would I do?"

"There's not going to be a burglar. Why would there be a burglar?"

"But that's what I feel."

"You can't blame it all on him. You chose to marry him. You're both to blame for your problems."

"You're wrong," Debra says, but Victoria wonders if her father had offered to help her get help so he would not have to only have Debra around.

When the house is quiet at three in the morning, Victoria chats online with her ex-boyfriend, Brennan, an aspiring stand-up comedian, relentlessly ambitious. They'd dated for six months in college. Now, he pays his bills writing puns for a joke T-shirt company in New York City. Victoria stays awake and helps him brainstorm. *Suicide is for quitters. You say potato, I say potato.* A T-shirt that says *Pants.*

Brennan must have loved Victoria once, and perhaps he still does, but he thought he might screw the sadness out of her, fix her with passion. They fucked on the floor and on his desk, Victoria's head knocking into the low-sloped ceilings of the room. She let him fuck her however he wanted, and though she did not always enjoy the sex, she cared for him, and it was better than being alone. She let Brennan go on trying to fix her until he grew exhausted, like she knew he would. Now, as friends, it feels good to flirt with him again. They chat until dawn light enters through the window, until the morning birds begin to sing.

"The baby birds are singing here," she says.

"Why are you up so late, young lady?"

"I had to make sure the birds made it safely through the night."

"That's the sweetest thing I've ever heard."

They exchange good mornings instead of good-nights. After he's gone, she misses him, and thinks it's so easy to make a person feel a certain way. Her nerves do something that make her want to cry.

At an outpatient facility for eating disorders, hidden at the edge of town, the waiting room walls are painted vomit-pink. Bouquets of cloth flowers collect dust next to stacks of wellness magazines. The patients, all women, move in slow motion. They sit stiffly and keep their eyes turned down. They do not smile, but Victoria smiles at each one, forcing the women's lips to curl up.

An intake nurse says Victoria should visit three times a week. Once for group therapy, once for the psychologist, and a final time for the nutritionist. The facility believes that the proper combination of therapy and drugs will help Victoria make progress.

"How much does it cost? Can you afford that?" Richard asks at dinner.

"You said you would help me if I came home."

"We are helping you by letting you stay here."

"Fine," Victoria says.

"You're an adult."

Upstairs, Victoria scans the Adult Gigs section of an online classifieds website, reading offers from men. Some are looking for blow jobs. Others seek big-assed girls to sit on their faces. One man wants an outgoing, good-looking, classy young woman for an exciting night of dinner, dancing, then we'll see where it goes, on me! Another seeks used panties while another wants a teen to wear a bikini and feather dust his shelves. The women who take these jobs must have a different set of nerves than Victoria. She is more interested in the men who call themselves artists, the ones looking for models for their work. Art Nude Model Wanted, she reads the headlines. SEEKING WOMAN FOR ARTISTIC PROJECT. LOOKING TO EXPAND PORTFOLIO. Model Sought for Artistic Nude Photographer. She wonders if he will be nude the entire time. Ha ha.

She emails, and in his reply, a man named Angelito describes himself as a photographer by passion and a cardiologist by profession, one of the best in the nation, he claims. He has worked for so long at the same hospital that he has earned regular weeks of leave. On his time off he makes all kinds of art, including photographs of naked women in his attic studio. He asks Victoria to bring with her items that reflect her personality.

"Anything that makes you you!" he says.

She packs a duffel bag with costumes and props. Second-hand paisley skirts, leotards, and pointe shoes unused for five years. She packs a velvet beret, love bead necklaces, an old concertina and a taxidermy mouse. She can't imagine how these items make her her.

When she comes downstairs, duffel in tow, she finds Debra starting in on her drinking early.

"The first third of my life was hell," Debra says. "I expected the last to be different. I want to be able to have a good time, but your father's always tired. I want to go dancing, go out, do things. But he always says his back hurts from driving."

"You should go dancing without him."

"You don't get it. It isn't the same. I want to do it with him."

Debra begins to cry, so Victoria places a hand on her back.

"I'm going to meet a friend. I'll be home later. Probably not for dinner."

"But you'll eat?"

"Yeah."

"If you want, if it's lonely upstairs, you can come sleep in my bedroom," Debra offers. "It'll be like a sleepover, if you want."

"That's okay." Victoria lifts her hand from her mother's shoulder. "I think I'm fine upstairs."

"Well, you can if you want, you know."

"I know."

Victoria takes the busy freeway into Massachusetts, to Angelito's home. She grips the steering wheel so hard that her hands turn white. She hopes her parasympathetic system will kick into gear, calm her tingly fight-or-flight feeling.

Even though she arrives ten minutes early, a fat, balding man is waiting at the door. He smiles and says, "Welcome to mi casa." He hugs Victoria like they are old friends, ushers her in, then tours her through his house. The walls are a gallery of Angelito's art. Splashed color landscapes and abstract designs. Cyanotype prints and found-object collage. A country landscape hangs above his bed, and a poster-sized photograph of a reclining naked woman is displayed on the opposite wall. Victoria thinks he must surround himself with his own art so he doesn't forget what makes him him.

After the tour, Angelito leads Victoria up a narrow flight of stairs to the attic, crowded with costumes, props, and books. On one side, a white backdrop, a tripod, and lights, set up and ready. But first, Angelito asks Victoria to take a seat on an antique chaise longue.

"What kind of model are you going to be?"

"I don't know," she says.

"There is fashion, and glamour, and art nude. Semi-nude. Erotica. Porn. I've tried shooting them all. How far are you planning to take this? Porn's where the money is. I've shot that too, but it wasn't for me."

"I'm just trying it out. I don't know what I'll do."

"I knew two girls who were going to do a couple porn films to pay for a backpacking trip through Europe. One of them chickened out, but the other one did it. And she got her trip. Think about it."

He unzips her bag of clothes and props, pulls out the items and examines them like an antiques dealer. He asks Victoria to change into a long paisley print skirt. She stands in front of the camera. The skirt comes off and she mimics the poses she has seen in magazines, sticks out a hip, points a toe. Bends to one side, then the other.

Angelito says, "Show me you! Be you!"

She feels silly and smiles, flings her arms, makes wild gestures. Angelito nods and laughs. Though he thinks this is Victoria being Victoria, it is only a cartoon impression, what she thinks he wants to see. Victoria thinks of a T-shirt that says, simply, *Angelito*.

After five hours of shooting, he puts down his camera. "Excellent." He hands Victoria four hundred dollars in crisp bills. "I'm sure we've got some good ones here. I'd love to shoot you regularly, every week, every other, if it suits you."

She drives home through Angelito's suburban neighborhood, then down a street lined with strip malls to get back to the highway. She stops at a convenience store to purchase snack cakes, bags of chips, candy bars, and sodas. She eats quickly in her car until her stomach is swollen, heavy. Stops again at a gas station to throw up what she ate.

On the highway, Victoria thinks, this is me being me. It's so easy to fool a person who thinks he knows what he knows.

She pays for group therapy with Angelito's money, the youngest of ten women around a plastic conference table. The frowning women who have been making progress for years exchange nervous glances. They have fitted themselves into costumes of superficial success: gold jewelry, blonde highlights, masks of unflattering makeup. But each looks on the verge of tears, like they saved up all their problems for this room.

It is Self-Image Day at the group meeting. A chipper college intern in a pantsuit smiles sweetly while trying to seem like an authority on female mental health. For this session's activity, she fans prints of famous paintings and portraits of women across the table. She asks the women to pick their favorite, then explain their choices to the group.

"I like this one because she's a woman but she looks like she could beat someone up."

"I like this one because it's just her head and shoulders."

"In this one, the woman seems like she's floating in tranquility."

Victoria does not have a favorite, so she picks the image nearest to her. "I like the landscape behind her. The tree and the sun."

"What all these women have in common," the intern says, "is they aren't extremely thin! They have real women's bodies. See, you don't have to be extremely skinny to be beautiful."

The patients leave in lighter moods, hopeful. But Victoria imagines they will grow progressively sadder until they meet next week for Healthy Choices Day. When only Victoria and the intern, who is packing her picture, remain, Victoria says, "Excuse me. I just wanted to mention."

The intern smiles as though she's expecting an expression of gratitude.

"The women in those picture might not be skinny, but they're still being objectified. They're still part of the male gaze. It's not like they have authority."

The intern's cheeks flush pink. "Okay," she says. "That's a good point I'll keep in mind."

Victoria decides she will not come back for Healthy Choices Day.

She creates a second name and email address. She carries secrets where they are safe, deep in the cavern of her chest. She drives to work for another photographer, a man named Christian who's much younger than Angelito. He is small and bald and wears tiny, round glasses. His studio space, in a large mill building, is more professional than Angelito's cluttered attic, and he does not tell Victoria to be Victoria. Instead, he directs her slightest gestures. The arch of her fingers. The angle of her hip. Victoria prefers Christian's style to Angelito's. She is better at following orders than being herself.

He sprays water on her white dress so it sticks to her skin. He takes photos, then asks her to take the dress off, change into just a long lacy skirt. She follows him into the mill building's basement and kneels sitting on the dirt floor. When he's done shooting, he writes her a check.

"Pretty face and good body. You could probably be

a semi-working model," he says. "I'd be willing to work with you again. I also shoot erotica. It pays more, if you're interested."

When Victoria returns the next week, Christian smears red lipstick around her nipples, ties her arms to her torso with a cord, puts a ball of waded fabric in her mouth. He lays her flat, and buckles a collar around her neck. He whips her, shoots her screaming. Victoria thinks of a T-shirt that says: *My other T-shirt is a rope.*

He pays her and thanks her after she has cleaned up.

"I'm available the rest of this month," she says, but Christian shakes his head.

"We've gotten what we can from each other. Time for you to go work for someone else."

"What's the deal?" Angelito asks, after their next shoot. He makes her a sandwich as she flips through a book of photographs by an artist she's never heard of. "Are you in a relationship?"

"There was this one guy, but he lives in New York now, and I'm not really sure if he's interested anymore."

"Not sure? If you're not sure then it's not happening. If he hasn't given you a ring by now, that's it. If I were him, with a girl like you, I'd snatch you up in a second."

Victoria eats the sandwich in small bites.

"I knew Meredith was the one right away. We've been married for fifty-two years. That's no small feat. It wasn't always easy, but you learn to honor each other's needs. The two things a person needs to transition into a functional adult is something to do and someone to love. Freud said that, and it's true."

Angelito stops Victoria's flipping at a picture of a childlike woman. Her eyes are closed and she is wearing only large white panties.

"Women don't wear plain white underwear any more. Do you have any plain white panties?"

"I don't think so," Victoria says.

"Shame."

Victoria sends Brennan some of Angelito's photos, the two she thinks make her look most attractive. In one, she is lying on her side on Angelito's chaise longue, staring darkly into the camera. The other is a profile of only her back.

Brennan replies: *Ouch! Look at you.* But he has also attached a photo, one he took of Victoria when they were dating. In the photo, she is lying on his bed, fully clothed and smiling. She looks calm, even healthy, like a normal human being. *Those pictures are nice, but I think this is my favorite.*

Victoria's nerves do something.

Downstairs, the house is dark except for a dim light coming from her parents' bedroom. Her father is out driving the taxi. She finds Debra asleep in bed. A duvet is draped loose around her legs. On the television, an infomercial is selling meal replacement shakes.

Victoria sits on the bed, looks at her mother, and pulls the duvet over her shoulders. She undresses, then pulls her body into her mother's bed.

"Goodnight," she whispers, and takes her mother's hand.

She looks for the remote, but when she can't find it she lets the television run. She props up the pillow, leans against the headboard and watches. The television is saying if you place an order they will double your order. If you buy right now, they will give you even more.

II

JAILBREAK

The husband and wife are in prison. The prison is warm and dark, like the inside of an animal. The prison guard is a little sick girl who will probably die in a matter of weeks. Already the girl is bedridden. She hardly speaks, but she has complained of terrible headaches. She does not eat, but has kindly decided to give her food to the husband and wife. Because she is too weak to carry the food herself, she ties plates to the dogs' backs, and the dogs wander down the halls to deliver the meals. The husband and wife need the food, but they are afraid of the dogs because the dogs may carry disease in the form of lice or ticks, perhaps the same disease that has afflicted the prison guard.

Sometimes the girl's cries and moans tear through the prison, and the prisoners wish these were the cries and moans of ghosts, not of a little girl. Ghosts cannot die, and the husband and wife are afraid of death. Until now, because the little girl brought food instead of death,

65

they had loved her. Sometimes, the wife believes the girl suffers from something with psychological origins, like anorexia. Plenty of girls suffer from anorexia when they are chronically unhappy, and the little girl has so much to be unhappy about. But the husband would wager, if he had any money, that the girl has been infected with Lyme disease.

The husband and wife do not discuss why they are in prison. Sometimes, when the wife feels like discussing it, she takes off her shirt, stuffs it in her mouth, and bites down hard. The husband misinterprets her nudity and gag as sexual advances. He walks to the wife, hugs her. He runs his hands down her back and kisses her.

When the husband feels like talking to the wife about why they are in prison, he distracts himself by thinking about sex. He thinks about sex until his wife takes off her shirt and shoves it in her mouth.

The husband and wife have no daughter of their own, and it would not be accurate to say they think of the prison guard as their daughter. But they do wonder about the origins of the prison guard. Who are her parents? Why did she end up here, serving prisoners? What, really, are the differences between a prisoner and a prison guard?

There are other activities the husband and wife do instead of talking about why they are in prison.

Wife: does a little dance in the corner of the cell involving small foot stomps. Bites off her fingernails, and tries to pluck the hairs between her eyebrows, but both the hairs and the nails are too short. Checks for lumps in her breasts. Uses dust to make drawings on the floor or walls. Practices yoga. Tries to imagine what God looks like.

Husband: closes his eyes and envisions various breakfast foods. Thinks about the sentences the wife says, and then repeats them backwards. Tries to fix his posture by standing up against the wall. Attempts to climb the stone walls. Writes songs and plays them on an air guitar. Tries to make himself laugh and then tries to make himself cry.

Both the husband and wife are getting very thin and frail. The food in the prison tastes like bland paste. The wife runs her hands along the ridges of her ribs and imagines she is a washboard. She thinks of fresh, soapy water. The husband has bad posture, and his thinness accentuates this. His body is beginning to look like an S.

It's a miracle! The little girl is up and walking. She stops at the bars of the wife and husband's cell.

"Hi," the wife says. "We thought you might be dead."

"Not quite," says the little girl. She looks at the floor and runs her hand along a rough metal bar. "But I'm getting pretty close, and it looks like you are too."

"Can't help it," says the husband. "Can you?"

"I don't know," says the little girl. "I don't think so."

"Can you please bring the keys?" the wife asks the girl. "It's not like we were supposed to die here. That wasn't the plan."

The little girl frowns. She doesn't remember the plan.

"When I was a little girl," the wife begins a short story, "I used to prefer to be by myself. In preschool, when we played outside, I wanted to sit alone and let dragonflies land on my fingers. There was a patch of wildflowers that always seemed to be full of dragonflies. I liked to climb a tree near the patch of wildflowers. I wanted to go up and up. Someone took my picture while I was standing in the tree. I was wearing a party dress and looked happy. I would show you the photo if I had it."

"Listen," the husband says, "Do you have the keys or what?"

The little girl looks down.

"Are they in your pocket?" the husband asks.

The little girl looks up, then back down.

"They're in her pocket," the husband says.

The husband lunges at the girl so fast that the wife falls over. He thrusts his arms through the bars and grabs the shoulders of the little girl. He pulls the little girl hard, and her shoulders and forehead knock against the bars with a heavy thunk. He shakes the girl back and forth with great force. Her head goes thunk thunk thunk on the bars, then her body is limp as a rag doll.

The wife says, "No." She closes her eyes and covers her ears and goes into the corner in a little ball and rocks rocks rocks. She hears the dogs run to the girl and start barking, but they are just medium-sized shaggy mutts and cannot do anything except bark. The wife has a vague feeling that this is madness, but another vague feeling that this is salvation.

The husband goes blind and deaf and strong as he smashes the girl's head into the bars. He sees a trickle of blood form on the girl's face. The girl's eyes are closed and her jaw slackens, but he won't stop because he needs to be humane and sure she is absolutely dead. He doesn't want her to suffer. He may have meant to ease the girl down gently onto the floor, but he lets go and her body drops.

"Can you get the keys?" the wife asks, still in a little ball, still not looking.

The husband says "Damn" and "Yes."

The wife hears the keys jangle and opens her eyes. She does not yet look at the husband or the girl. She just looks at the wall. "That was really bad," she says.

"Dammit," The husband says.

Both the husband and the wife had imagined

breaking out of the prison many times. Each time, their escape had been sweet and joyous, like a field of wildflowers brushing against a gently windblown sky. They imagined their escape would feel something like meeting their newborn child or discovering God.

UNLIKE ANY OTHER DAY

The man was having a day unlike any other day. It was a day of mornings. He woke up all day, stretched, looked in the mirror. It was a day of mirrors that glinted and refracted the morning light at odd angles. He poured himself coffee. It was a day of coffee but he was out of milk, and it wasn't a day of going to the store, so he drank the coffee black. It occurred to the man it was Friday again. It had been a week of Fridays. It was June again. A year of Junes.

He repeated the word June out loud until it had no meaning. The idea of June kept startling him. It was a day of startled moments. He was startled by the chandelier, which now sprouted from the floor. By his reflection in the light-shocked mirror, upside down instead of reversed. By the whale songs flowing out of birds' mouths or else the birds were tiny whales, surviving somehow out of water.

He remembered an exhibit at the aquarium as a

child. The exhibit was just two outlines of whales on a big wall, one inside the other. Both outlines symbolized life-size animals, only the larger outline represented a whale from many thousands of years ago and the smaller outline represented a whale of today. They were only lines on a wall, but the shrinking whale had startled him so deeply that he must have never fully recovered.

Another exhibit, another museum. Natural History. Behind glass, life-size models of a what men and women looked like as cave people. Bodies like lean humans, but apish faces with jutting mouths and clunky cheeks. Long, dirty hair. The cave people looked on at some far-off threat beyond the wall of the exhibit, a lion or computer-age technology. It was that their hair looked like homeless people's hair. It was that they were so small and naked and vulnerable and looked-at through a pane of glass. He felt small and naked and vulnerable too.

It was a day of calling his mother. Each time he woke and called his mother she said, "Oh son, you're just having a day. No problem. Take a breath."

He was distracted from the conversation by the feeling and then the sight of a tiny beetle walking across his chest. I am a bodyscape for beetles, he thought. It was a day of wanting to be painted by some artist who painted bodyscapes, wanting to be hung on the wall of a museum.

His mother repeated, "Just breathe."

He breathed. It was a day of breathing, which made it more like other days than not, but he did not want to think about that for too long. What if tomorrow he got stuck in a day full of moments between breaths?

"Don't worry," his mother said. "You're okay."

It was a day of love for his mother. She tried her best.

"There," she said. "A good many people have not come this far."

She said it like a victory, but he heard it like a loss.

THE LAST DAY OF SCHOOL

On the last day of school, it occurred to the old teacher, as she walked home, that she no longer wanted to give or receive any information she could not use. The poor couple at four a.m. the night before who reduced themselves to singular monsters as they argued on the street. Public radio's ticker tape of tragedies and gloat. The distance from Earth to the moon, from the moon to the end of the universe. She did not want to know when the sun will extinguish itself in a blast of cold forgetting or why she could not forgive her mother. She did not want to listen to adolescent drama, nor did she want to tell teenagers what was best for them.

The orange cat that her neighbor fed got hit by a car or else went crazy. He dragged his paralyzed hind legs up the stone stairs of the schoolteacher's home, like a wilted flower tittering on its stalk. The cat wanted nothing to do with the woman, and moved under the porch faster than she thought a paralyzed animal should be able to move. Anyone living is the enemy of the dying.

She left the cat and went inside to call the humane society. The woman on the other end put her on hold, then she heard the recorded message from the animal control department, "We are not here. We never were. If you have an emergency or someone is in immediate danger, ask yourself: what is the value of danger?"

She decided it was in her best interest to forget about the cat. She walked down the street to where children infested the city park. They played happily until a larger, more violent child showed up. His name was Pete, and he said he was the devil. He chased the other kids and cut swing ropes. He poured sand down the backs of shirts and lifted girls' skirts.

"I'm here," he said, "and my mother loves me. Don't believe the lies." He used a child language she didn't fully understand to whisper in her ear. Something about the meaning of life, and why it doesn't really matter.

The old school teacher went home and waited for her husband to arrive. By waiting, I mean, she swept the wood floor, folded laundry and looked up a recipe to use on the chicken in the fridge. Her autonomic functions were hard at work. She fell asleep on the couch and had a sexually charged dream.

The dream was about a former lover. Everything was

perfect. She was young, so was he. They stood on the top of a mountain. They kissed and talked, felt infinite with wisdom, like two birds just birthed. In view: a ridgeline, then a sky so magic with color she should have known it was only a dream.

When she woke hours later, she felt angry with loss, and her husband was there next to her, waking up too.

"I had a dream," he said. "We were standing on top of a mountain. We had all the information and knew all the answers. In view: a ridgeline, and then a sky so magic with reds and oranges that I knew you were sleeping next to me in the waking life."

His was a sexually charged dream, so he crawled on top of the old schoolteacher and ran his hand down her body. She was angry with loss, but she did not say. After they made love, she felt better. She felt like a giant had stomped out all her want. She was thin, and solid as a hatchet.

THE CYCLOPS HAS HIS REASONS

T he siren and the cyclops had been taking a lovely drive before a night of dinner, drinks, and then, you know. They were incredibly in love. They rolled past the strip malls, driving happily, letting themselves believe the soft love songs that played on the radio, as though they were high school sweethearts.

He was smiling blissfully and admiring her pretty blond hair, so she thought she would take the opportunity (because he could be such a tyrant with his opinions) to carefully explain the reasons why she was so opposed to placing blame.

"There are always reasons people do the things they do," the siren said. "Like, extremists and terrorists wouldn't hate us if we hadn't spread our consumerist Hollywood agenda all over their world. The Somali pirates wouldn't have pirated if foreign fishermen didn't rob their waters."

The cyclops thought about her words for many

minutes, clenching and softening his fists. "I see how that makes sense," he said. He drove on in thoughtful silence. She extended her arm out the open window and felt thick, warm air pulse across her skin.

"Like my father!" The cyclops burst, punching the steering wheel with both fists. "He hates so many people! Like gays and Muslims and homeless bums! It's infuriating. He never thinks about what makes people how they are."

The siren smiled sweetly to herself, and then at the cyclops. "Yes," she said, "that's terrible. But remember, there has to be reasons why your father is hateful and small-minded. Who knows what his childhood was like?"

"Oh," said the cyclops, "I see, I see. Something made him that way." His tight jaw slacked and he leaned back and relaxed. He thought the siren must be the most beautiful, empathetic creature.

The siren thought (now that the cyclops had accepted her perspective) he would have to understand that there are reasons why she did what she did too.

He paid for her dinner at the downtown restaurant, then danced with her at a local bar where he became quite drunk. She drove him to a hotel. She undressed him and made love to him like a wild beast. He shot five orgasms through his body before he fell asleep. She left him there to return to her husband and forget all about the cyclops.

Instead of understanding, the cyclops broke into her home, lifted her by the neck, and smashed her face into the wall until she did not have a face.

TWO DOGS

I was on employment insurance, out of work, having trouble structuring my day. Then my mind halved itself and inhabited two dogs. One of the dogs was a dirty stray, the other a house pet, small and trained.

As a house pet, I loved more than I ever thought possible, I followed and obeyed. I lay on the ground like a fallen flower petal. A hand passed over my belly. I paused for a collar. I ate what the masters ate. Only, I ate it from a bowl on the floor.

As a stray, I wandered. I associated with many alleyways, many squirrels and birds. I followed scents. I crouched and stalked. I stalked another stray dog. I fucked it. I felt my consciousness dissolve. I followed a homeless man and called him my pack. Neither of us were the alpha. Neither of us were the dog. We were the rain, the snow, the buildings built up in this city like inhabitable gravestones, marking a history we had no need for.

Then the stray dog found and fucked the house pet. It was the most natural thing, fucking myself. It felt like walking into a pool of water the exact same temperature as the air. But the house pet's owner hit me when he found me, and I split apart again.

Do you visit a place like this? A place where two dogs meet but it happens so quickly and ends so violently, you're certain it doesn't count?

BROCKVILLE, 1972

What is this? Where's that music coming from? Across the street? Oh. Here. What is this, some kind of New Orleans Restaurant? Expensive. Oh, excuse me. Oh, yuck. I do not like you. What is that cleavage? Is he wearing a gold necklace? Oh. What is this? N'awlins? A-New-Orleans-Restaurant. Hm. Oh, the menu's in the window. Expensive. Well, I don't know where else to go. I don't know. One drink. Hi. It's just me. Nobody's coming besides me. Party of one, please. Is this New Orleans food? Oh, beads. Thank you. Beads are pretty. They match my outfit, maybe? Mardi Gras beads. Fun. I'll just put them in my purse, or I'll wear them. I quit my counseling class today. No more. I liked the little children patients, but I'm no good at the school part. I like working with the kids, though, and I'm good at it too. They have what's called autism. So sad. They don't like it in the hospital. It isn't nice for them. One sweet little girl I worked with, she looked at me and said, I want pretty clothes like yours!

She was wearing a paper dress. She said, I want to have a pretty dress like yours. And I get it. Every little girl wants to be pretty. I hate hospitals. So depressing. Everyone's sick and the smells! And I didn't like the nurses either, saying I couldn't teach her how to tie her shoes. It's useless, they said. Waste of time. I can't do the tests, though, in class. No way! I threw the tests away and walked out. I'm just no good at all that.

Oh, huh? Yes. The bar is fine. What? My other ear. I'm deaf in this ear. Oh, those people kissing don't look nice. Kissing in a restaurant? That's disgusting. Is his hand up her skirt? Oh, he's disgusting. He's got no hair. And she's fat! He could put his hand on a fat girl like that? Daddy has thinning hair now. But he's handsome.

Not fat and all. He's a real dreamboat. He used to be a real stud. Yeah, thinning hair, but he's still handsome. He's Italian, and classy. Not like these people. Hi, yes. Oh, no I haven't looked at the menu yet. Let's see. Hm. Okay. I need to decide! Menu. What are these? Tequila sunrise. I like bourbon! Daddy likes bourbon. I don't know. Hm. I don't know what these drinks are. Hello. Excuse. Excuse me. Do you have bourbon? I don't know what kind. What does the bottle look like? Let me see. Let me see. Oh, anything. What is the rocks? Ice. Let's see. On the rocks is fine. Or, what other way do you make it?

Oh, hello. Me? Two men want to talk. I am attractive.

They're not, but that's okay. I can talk. It's not like I'm
going to kiss them or anything. No way. Are you drinking
bourbon too? Don't mind my hair. I need to cut it. Do
you like it? I hope my sister Victoria didn't cut her hair
that ugly way she said she would. It's stylish, she said, but
it won't look pretty so short. Not on her. I said, what do
you want to be ugly for? It would be so ugly. How would
she wear clips in it? She would look like a boy. My hair's
short, but I need it that way. I don't look good with long
hair. No way! Short like Twiggy. Pixie. That's what they
call it, a pixie cut. Do you like short hair? Oh, no? I like
to be stylish, like Twiggy, and I'm skinny, like Twiggy
too. So what if I'm skinny? Twiggy is skinny. People don't
call her chicken-legs. People don't throw garbage at her,
like they did to me in elementary school. Kids are so
mean. Oh. Thank you. It's bourbon right? Right, okay.
I've never been here before! It's New Orleans food, right?
That's good because I like food spicy. Daddy likes to eat
whole chilies, and I do too. Yeah, real spicy. The hotter,
the better. Hot, hot, that's how I like it. He ate whole
chilies from our garden before he lost everything. Dump
we live in now, no garden.

Oh. Hm. Good drink. I don't know. This is bourbon?
Strange. What is this? Oh, bourbon. I'm not sure I like this.
Why are these men laughing? Not cool. What's funny?
Not good looking, anyways, those men. Disgusting how

fat people can let themselves get. Nobody in my family is fat, thank God. Double chin. Nasty. What? My name? Oh, it's Thora. Mmm. Hmm. What? What! Yes l like it. It's bourbon! It's, well. Well, I don't want to drink it fast. I like to take my time. What? I can't hear. My daddy drank bourbon. He's an artist. At least he would have been, but he never followed through. He studied at Toronto School of Design. He was a real lady's man. Really, like. He had a beautiful voice, too. Sang like Frank Sinatra or Dean Martin. Better, even. Do you sing? He cut a record once, and he was supposed to bring it to the big producers. The music hotshot producers in New York City, but he never followed through! I have the record. And my mother, she was in the Royal Canadian Air Force. Like my father was too, only he was in a submarine. The military, I mean. He was in the military, I mean, not the Air Force. He was in the submarines, and it almost got hit by a missile, the one he was in. It's true! I wouldn't be here if that happened.

But my mother, she used to be fine before she went crazy. I don't know what kind of crazy she was, but I was scared. What! Sorry, what? I can't hear you. I'm deaf in one ear. She died of cancer, but before that she went crazy. What? Sorry! It's a good thing I wear glasses, you say. Because I am one ugly person. Oh. Hm. Well, that's what you think.

I'm not the ugly one. They're ugly. Yeah, so ugly. They were ugly. Fat and disgusting and real pigs. With no class. No class at all. I got class. No one in this town's got class. They don't even know what class is. My family has got class. In eighth grade, when the professional from the beauty school came in to look at us girls and give beauty advice, it was me he said it to, me who could be a model. He looked at me and said, who cut your hair? Me, I said. I did. And he said, it's perfect.

This city is full of lowlifes. Look at these properties. No upkeep. Broken walkways to the doors, ugly colors painted on the houses. Who would choose to paint their house that bright red color, or that dirt color there? I want a big, contemporary house with lots of windows. Frank Lloyd Wright is my favorite. Grandpa once built a house designed by one of his students, before Daddy lost everything. Nothing doing here. Too many old people, retiring and getting ready to die. How depressing. Too many noisy, disrespectful kids. People don't know how to take care of their things. Is that a car with no bumper? Oh, they got to fix that. Nope, nothing doing. I'm going to Ann Arbor. That's where the life is. Ann Arbor is swinging! That's where it's going on! And the men there, they're sexy! I'd. You know, with them. Well. No, I wouldn't. I'm only kidding. One day. After I'm married. If the men aren't like these men. I'm not the ugly one, that's for sure.

Wait. Wait. Am I going the right way? Wait—am I going the right way? I think I am. I'm not sure. Wait. Huh. Where's the river? No, I must be going the right way. Or, did I go too far? Shit. Where am I?

Daddy and Nanny are going to wonder where I've been. They'll be mad. Oh well. I'm twenty-six. Not like I haven't been out of the house before. Not like I haven't been other places, that's for sure. Daddy was pissed as hell last year when me and Victoria went with those Muslims to Montreal all night. Oh, he didn't like that. Faiz and his friends. Oh, he was pissed as hell when we got home. He said, you don't go defying me! He knew. He knew what men were like, because he was like that himself. Yip! Lady chaser. He was with the women, that's for sure. All we did was sit in that room and talk for hours. All those men talking about philosophy for hours! And smoking cigarettes. The whole room was filled with smoke. I kept gagging, couldn't even breathe. Felt like I was going to pass out. Now Victoria's gone and married Faiz. She wears those Muslim outfits now. She's brainwashed! Two kids already, and he's got her working like a dog. For them, the woman is like the slave of the family. And she's white, so that's even worse. She's a slave to the whole family—all those in-laws. Two kids and she says she wants more. They've got a house, she says, and a car, but I don't buy that her life is so hot. He proposed to me first, but I said, No way! I wasn't into that. No way. I made friends with him in a class, because he looked all alone, but I wasn't going to marry him. No way. Nanny said he married her for a green card. Now he's talking about moving all his relatives over from Pakistan. She says she loves him and she's happy, but I don't buy that! Oh, she's brainwashed, for sure.

Oh, I know where I am. My street. Yes. Good this is my street. Knew I'd make it. Is this right? Is this my street? Yes, there's the apartment. There's the apartment. Good. Yes. Home, home. Shitty apartment. Oh well. What are those kids doing? Those kids! Playing in front of the apartment, again. How many times am I gonna have to tell them? Oh, with their footballs. Trampling the flowers. Get out of there! Oh, for Christ's sake, balls lost in Nanny's flowers again. Damned kids. Hey! Get out of there! Don't walk in there! You're breaking our flowers! Forsynthia! Go play in your own yard. Good for nothing, stomping through the plants. Disrespectful. Calling me names. Kids said I was ugly when I was little. Frog eyes and chicken legs. But I wasn't ugly. I can't help if I am ugly. My mom drank when she was pregnant, that's why. That's what they said, those doctors. Oh well. Everyone thinking I was stuck up, too. Hating me. But I wasn't stuck up, just ashamed of where we lived. We used to have money. Rich, like. Real rich. But then we lost it all. Daddy ran all Grandpa's businesses into the ground. All those luxury apartments by the river. One designed by a student of Frank Lloyd Wright. Dirt poor. It wasn't all his fault. He was an artist, but that's what happens, the son takes on the family business. Ran it all into the ground. We moved into a one-room, unheated apartment, borrowed from a family friend. It's so sad. We slept on lawn chairs. That's embarrassing. Like, yeah, I was so embarrassed. Amelia came over once, but that was different. She had a huge nose and a missing leg, and a grossly crooked nose. Oh Jesus. She could come over. But not the others. Hey! I told you, don't play in front of our house. The next time I find a ball in the garden, I'm going to take it! You're ruining all the flowers. Hey! Don't they know that flowers are like people? Living and breathing and being good?

Door's open, but Daddy isn't home. Nanny's probably asleep. Dark in here. Oh well. Dark's when I've seen Mommy's ghost, there in the kitchen. In front of the sink, washing dishes. She was standing facing the sink last time I saw her. I'm not scared though. She comes to me. I see ghosts. Supernatural things happen like that. I say, I love you, Mommy, even though you didn't want me. They say something changed in you after the electroshock, and I believe it. I don't know what was wrong with you, but the electroshock didn't work. Nanny says you didn't love me, and I think she was right, because I remember being three years old, back when you were still here, and Nanny asked me what chair I wanted to sit in, and I said, that one, the big one in the corner with the tall back, so I can hide from Mommy. Oh well. Lights. Where's the switch? Other wall. I keep forgetting.

I wonder if Daddy is trying to find some work? Work. Yeah. Work would be good. He needs to work. I tell him. I say, you need to work. What are you doing all day, and he says, finding a job! I'm working. I'm looking for work. You're working? I say. Yeah, I'm working. You're working. Okay. Good. Hope it's something he can keep this time. Not some rich woman with a husband, or whoever. Lights on, good. Oh, is it a mess in here? No mess. Good. Nanny's gonna be mad I didn't help clean. Man at the bar. I'm not ugly. Oh, the blanket's on the floor. Who did that? I'll pick it up. Phew, what a dump. But it's better than the last place. Sleeping on lawn chairs for ten years. No way I'm going back to that.

I'll kill myself first. I'm done with school. I can't do it. I hate the people there, but I'll find a way to make money. And I'll get out of this town. Where's Nanny? Asleep. She's going to be angry. Quiet up the stairs. Peek in. Yes, asleep. Snoring. Oh ugly, her foot sticking out the bed. The hard part of her foot! So ugly. She should use a lotion on her feet, too. Like I tell her. Like I keep telling her. What Nanny? What was that? No. He isn't home, but there were those damn kids playing in the yard again. I told them to fuck off! No, I don't know who their parents are. No respect, though. Snoring again. Hate that! Hate that sound.

Downstairs to the couch and pillow. Bed, bed. I'm tired. Have to wash my face, though. Always wash my face. With warm water and a washcloth. Skincare. And have to wear sunscreen, too, or else I'll get ugly black blotches like Mommy had. So disgusting. Melanoma. That's what it's called. Big black ugly blotches like base-balls. When I was little, Nanny said Mommy was dangerous, so when I saw her on the street, I ran away. I was so scared. She was calling my name, and trying to give me candy. I ran. I ran like crazy, oh yeah! Sunscreen. Always. Gotta wear it.

Wash my face, and then bed, but I'll keep the light on. No. Turn the light off. No. But when I turn the light off, I can see pictures of her, and screaming in my mind. But when I keep the lights on, the light comes through my eyelids, and I wonder if you can still see light through your eyelids after you're dead.

I keep thinking, oh my poor Daddy. It was disgusting, once. I couldn't believe what he did. I wanted to puke.

Pigeon. I said, you fed us pigeon? Because he didn't tell us he'd killed a pigeon for our dinner until a year after the fact. Oh that's so dirty, isn't it? That's disgusting. Taxi driver, careful of the road. That's a red light. Yes, you see it. I wouldn't have eaten it! I would have spit it out! What speed have you been going? Too fast? I think the turn is coming up. Or isn't it? They'll hire me at N'awlins if they know what's good for them. I could be a waitress, that's for sure. And I'll save my money and get us out of here. I wouldn't tell this to anyone, about the pigeon. It's so gross, it's so gross. But I'm telling you now. You're a good driver. I trust you. I don't mind that you're ethnic. A lot of ethnics are criminals, but I don't believe that all of them are, you know. Do you like it here better than where you were before? Oh, born in Brockville? I hate this town. No class, you know? You probably want to get out too! Oh. Yes. Here's good. Okay.

I'm not going back to school. No way. They'll just have to do without me. I've got something else to do. Big plans. I can work. I can do that. I'm good with people, most people. The nice ones. To hell with the others. I can work here, at N'awlins. I can hold a lot at once in my hands. I've got big, long piano fingers, though I never learned to play piano. Someday, I hope to have a piano in my house. A keyboard would be good enough. I have a natural ear for music, I think. I could hold many plates of food at one time, but

I don't know about taking orders. If I could write them down that would be good. And the noise in here might not be good for my deaf ear. I could take dishes away. I could set tables. I could wash dishes if I had to, for the money. I'm looking for the owner! What? You're the owner? I'm looking for the owner. Oh, you are. Drinking, though? Oh well. Oh, it's water? I'd like to work here are you hiring. I'm a hard worker and people like me. I'm good with setting tables, and I can carry a lot. What! Start now? Well, okay. I can go around with water, ask people if they want more. I can refill the bread baskets. What!

That pitcher of water there on the bar? Oh thank you. Take it to the tables, yes, I see. Table to table, filling water glasses, being helpful. Hi. Would you like some water? Some more water, I mean? Oh, your glass is full. I was looking at your other glass. Sorry. Your beer glass is what I was looking at.

How is everything with your meal? Good, good. Oh, that looks good. What is it? Shrimp. Oh, crawfish, some kind of shrimp. We used to eat shrimp in pasta all the time. Okay. Good. Well, good. Hello! Would you like some more water? Let me just, sorry, it isn't polite to reach. Oh thank you. Oh, napkin on your lap dear, right? It's important to keep things nice. You don't want to spill. Hello. Good evening everyone. Can I serve you more water? I love your red hair. So beautiful! I am going to have a daughter who has red hair. I know it. My favorite doll had red hair. I named her Red Head. Where are you from? Oh, Mexico! I'd love to go to Mexico. Drink margaritas on the beach. What? Oh, Mexico, New York. I didn't know white people lived in Mexico, but I hear the beaches are like parties, yeah! Sorry? Oh, Mexico, New York. Okay. Those waiters over there at the bar are having a real good time! Laughing. I'll wave to them. Hi! They're testing me, to see, and I'll show them why they ought to hire me.

What! Come outside? Okay. But I'm working. Yes, sure. But who are you? The owner? But that man is the owner. You must be co-owners, then? Just the owner? Oh. Who was that man who said I could work? What! A barfly! I can't believe it. Oh, I'm so embarrassed. That is so rude. But I did good, though. I know I did. I can do a lot of things. I can hold a lot of dishes, and I'm good with people too. You just need to speak to them, you know. I was working with an autistic girl in the hospital, trying to teach her to tie her shoes, and the nurses all told me not to waste my time. But I kept working with her, kept working, like this—showing her how to make the loops, talking real sweet, and then one day, she did tie her shoe, she did it. The nurses were amazed. They never thought she could learn. But I knew she could. Yeah! It's like what I said, you just have to speak to them right. You just got to get on their level.

THE TALL, THIN MAN

A tall, thin man came to the city. He crossed the bridge in the middle of the darkest night of the year. The moon had eaten itself three days ago, and the crumbs left over looked like weak stars.

Sadness had set in to the cracked brains of people here, the way a building softens at the corners. I had packed my bags and was carrying my suitcase to the bus station, but the sight of the man halted me. I turned around, went home, wondered about the nature of hope.

In the morning, the tall man went door to door, passing out gifts. He said, "These gifts are your new moons." He gave an old woman a set of salt and pepper shakers, shaped like clones. He gave a little boy a Native American headdress. He gave a pair of newlyweds a long rope ladder. He gave me a tall coatrack with brass hooks. To each person, he spoke the very same words: "You are living in my dream."

By noon a crowd assembled around the fountain, in

front of city hall. The tall, thin man stood in the center of the crowd, as though he were a planet and the people were his moons. The people all held their gifts like weapons, and the old woman threw her salt and pepper shakers at his head. The little boy held his headdress around the man's neck. The newlyweds whipped him with their rope ladder. I waited, clutching my coatrack, for somebody to stop me. By the end of the day, the man had gone black. And we all cried, our grief was so deep.

Along the bottom of the fountain, tiny wildflowers grew. Some were purple. Some were so yellow we mistook them for gold. I knew that I would miss them. I went home and found my suitcase, still packed. Still full of gifts I would one day give to other people, in some city far away that I would never understand.

EVERYTHING WAS QUICKSAND

The tables were quicksand. The chairs quicksand. The coffee and the coffee pot were quicksand. The car was quicksand. The cat melted into the cat, then the floor. The floor melted into the earth, which was quicksand. The buildings were quicksand, though they took decades to melt into themselves. The engagement ring my husband got from his mother and gave to me was quicksand. It melted off my finger.

My husband watched like, I wish I knew how to save her, how to slow her squirming, calm her restless mind. How to bottle her up. But the bottles were all quicksand so he indulged in what some might call his perverse tendency to watch and do nothing. He was not sure what exactly I was sinking into, other than myself. He was not sure where my self began and ended.

Forever is not so frightening on a grand scale, but small forevers are another story. The forever between two grains of sand. The tiny forever between zero and one. Maybe as I sank he watched and did nothing because he was stuck in the space between his one thought and another. Maybe he knew I would manage on my own.

I stilled my limbs the way a baby figures out its balance. I took a steady breath and another. I slowly rose. What would he have done if I had needed his help in this moment of my own salvation? He had a stick. He had his hand and his doubts. But his doubts were quicksand. And his hand? And the stick.

AN EXERCISE IN ETIQUETTE

Everything that summer felt like an exercise in etiquette. The publisher of the Maple Leaf Press, the community newspaper that operated out of a crumbling barn in southern New Hampshire, decided to handle their financial losses by cutting the staff. Eleanor was the first to go. She sat in front of her editor's desk watching Jane's chin double as she spoke. Jane gave Eleanor a month's notice. They both fingered cups of chamomile tea and Jane prattled on about how the Maple Leaf Press wasn't a lone soldier. Print journalism was being slammed all over. Jane's face looked tugged. Her orange hair puffed out in all directions.

"You have a future," she told Eleanor, pitching forward over the desk. A lock of frizzy hair dipped into her tea.

Everyone has a future, Eleanor thought, but she just said, "Thank you."

She had worked at the paper for exactly one year,

and because she still did not feel attached to the job, she was not upset about the news. She had spent the year driving from school board meeting to library commission meeting, from fourth-grade play to Veterans Day memorial ceremony. Sitting at her final selectman's meeting in the whitewashed town hall, Eleanor took diligent notes. She propped her voice recorder on an empty chair. She liked to be thorough and precise, overprepared. She liked to transcribe entire meetings, to whittle through the ums and likes of speech. The Maple Leaf Press did not merit the trouble, but it kept her focused and engaged.

She jotted down key phrases as the three selectmen bantered on in front of an audience of five. They discussed a dead raccoon, which, for three months, waste management had failed to scoop off of the main road. They bickered about the location of this year's annual golf ball drop, and how they might remedy the problem of ducklings toppling down the sewer grates, breaking their necks. The two oldest selectmen, Harvey Daniels and Heather Perkins were both wizened and each nearing eighty years old. On nearly every issue, they fervently disagreed with the newest and youngest of the three.

"We need to think about efficiency," Alec Rimmon liked to say about budgets. He stood and planted his hands wide across the table. His fingers spread and turned white from the pressure of his body. "A corporation would do it my way. We need to think. We need to run this town like a business."

"A town is not a business. It is town," the two dinosaurs rebutted in unison.

Eleanor knew only a little about Alec. He was glossy to the point of grease. In a past life he was a high-powered businessman. His thick white hair swept severely to one side and didn't move as he spoke. His sharp blue eyes and upright posture, his waxy care was unusual in small-town politics. In his own way, he was at least as absurd as the two older selectmen.

Eleanor's stomach hurt and acid burned in her throat as it gripped its way up from her gut. The inside of her body always worked this way, now. Broken. She dressed professionally for these meetings. A blazer, a clean sweater, a collared shirt. She wore her only pair of high-heeled shoes, though she walked clumsily in them, and took her heels out when she sat.

She sat stiffly in the almost-empty room, jotting mechanically. Her green eyes flipped up to the selectmen, down at her notes. She had a strong jawbone and deep brown hair. She wore no makeup. Strangers and acquaintances, unprompted, sometimes commented on her looks. She hated the way people behaved as though beauty were something valuable. She felt as though, at any moment, she would turn sour, rot, let people down. But she just said, "Thank you" when a compliment came her way.

At the meeting, she smiled or furrowed her brow at the moments when these gestures seemed appropriate.

When the three-hour meeting came to a close, the five townspeople in the audience stood, ambled, small-talked. Where would they go now? Eleanor scanned her notes for the phrases she had circled or underlined, bits of information that needed clarification or better quotes. She waited until a last lonely townsperson shuffled out the double door, then approached Alec Rimmon. She could have approached any of the selectmen, but Alec had a way of encouraging communication. He returned her calls and was rarely sarcastic. He smiled when he answered her questions.

"Well, thank you," she said, after she'd finished asking him her questions. She pushed her recorder and notebook into her purse, pulled an arm through the sleeve of her coat.

He watched her. "It's a shame to hear you're leaving us."

She agreed it was a shame.

"I'll tell you what. Why don't I take you to lunch to thank you for your good work?"

"That would be nice."

"Wonderful. Are you a pickup truck or Mercedes girl? I could get my wife's Mercedes for the day."

"I've never ridden in a Mercedes before."

"Okay, kiddo. Mercedes it is."

After the Maple Leaf Press hired Eleanor, she and her boyfriend Nicholas moved into a cottage on the banks of Sunrise Lake. The cottage was zoned as a seasonal vacation home, but Eleanor and Nicholas lived there even during the iciest months of the year. The one small wall heater couldn't warm the cottage's two rooms. Besides the combined bedroom and living room, the kitchen held a half-size oven and a half-size refrigerator. The bathroom resembled a tiny, one-man space capsule.

Nicholas worked nights attending to a halfway house. Eleanor spent the time he was gone reading and drinking wine until she had consumed enough to fall asleep. Other nights, she drove out to the Main Street convenience store, picked up bags of chips, ice cream, microwave dinners, and individually wrapped snack cakes. She unwrapped the first cakes in the car, continued unwrapping in the house. Later, she vomited in a trash bag. Sometimes, on Nicholas' days off, they took their cross-country skis across the lake or drove out of town to see a movie. Some Saturdays, she visited her mother, Mary, at the Deerfield Assisted Living Center.

On the days Nicholas did not work, he stayed buried in the blankets of their bed until noon, his wiry body stretched flat. He woke and strummed a guitar, belted the songs he'd written in college. Eleanor paced and looked out the windows and felt claustrophobic. She looked at Nicholas and looked away, and looked at him again. She told Nicholas she was going to the library to work, but drove to fast food restaurants to order off dollar menus and vomit in the bathroom stalls. She came home sedated and sore.

Eleanor enjoyed living on Sunrise Lake. The town was manageable, contained. People recognized and greeted her when they saw her. It could have been that Sunrise Lake was becoming a kind of home.

But the same week that the Maple Leaf Press gave Eleanor her notice, Nicholas found a new job as an employment specialist at a refugee resettlement agency. The agency's headquarters were forty minutes northwest, in the city where they both grew up. Nicholas' parents, Martin and Dawn, still lived there. He suggested the couple move into his parents' home, to save money.

"It's closer to my work," he said. "And your job's ending. It just makes sense."

"It makes sense," Eleanor said.

Nicholas and Martin renovated the damp basement. They rewired and hung drywall and painted. They rolled carpet over cement and hung curtains over tiny windows. Eleanor helped Dawn attack the basement's clutter, the remnants of Nicholas' childhood, stuffed into cabinets, piled up and dusty. Grade school assignments and hand-drawn cards. Participation ribbons and basketball trophies. Scratched CDs and tangled cassettes. Dawn chuckled and gushed, when she found these relics. She thrust each of Nicholas' drawing towards Eleanor, who was expected share in the delight.

When they moved, Eleanor made an agreement with herself to stop throwing up. It would be a courtesy to Dawn and Martin. It would be too difficult to hide. Some days, Eleanor stayed in the basement, in bed for hours, salivating over imagined feasts. Others, when fantasy failed, she shook with anxiety. She smoked cigarettes and left her desk to take long runs through the suburban streets in the newly developed neighborhoods nearby, their streets line with identical McMansions.

Or else she forced herself to concentrate on the pain of deprivation, sweating, telling herself to fall in love with the void.

Some mornings, she was still half asleep when Nicholas kissed her on the forehead, before leaving for work.

"Promise to be good?" he said.

"I promise," she said.

"Do you promise?" he said, and she said, "I promise."

The day before her lunch arrangement with Alec, Eleanor took the back roads to the Deerfield Assisted Living Center. The back roads calmed her. She liked rolling over the hills, through the trees, textured with cinematic light and shadow. She listened to the radio, smoked cigarettes, rested her arm on the window.

She was suddenly horny. She was pleased with herself for feeling horny. It was rare. She could finally be the one to instigate sex with Nicholas.

She texted him: I want sex!

He texted back: Wait!

She parked her car in the near-empty lot in front of the center, told herself to keep her temper in the face of her mother. At the front desk, the fat, bored high school student put down her cell phone and signed Eleanor in.

Eleanor walked down the yellowing hallway, pressed open Mary's door.

The room smelled both sterile and sour, like Lysol sprayed across urine stains and left to dry. Mary sat stiffly on a twin-sized bed caged by aluminum rails. She stared at the wall opposite the bed. Her knotted hair formed a nest above her head. Eleanor wondered how she came to look so old. A pretty nurse pushed open the door and placed a set of towels on the room's unused armchair. Her gait mimicked the movement of the residents, heavy and sedated.

Mary's right leg was wrapped in medical dressings. She had slipped on the bathroom floor and snapped her femur. Eleanor picked up the towels from the chair, sat, kept the towels on her lap. She forced herself to look at her mother.

"How are you feeling?"

"They put a twelve-inch titanium rod in there." Mary pointed to her leg.

"You're part bionic," Eleanor said. She pictured Mary's metal rod, years after Mary had died, shining and strong in the ground. They sat for many moments in silence.

"You look stressed," Mary said, alert now, peering at her daughter.

"I'm not stressed. You always say that."

"Don't worry about losing your job. You'll find

another. You're so young, and you have skills. You have so much more opportunity than I've ever had. Are they doing anything nice for you at the paper before you go?"

"No."

"I can tell you're stressed."

"I'm not stressed. Stop saying that."

"You look it. I can tell you are. What do you have to be stressed about. Twenty somethings, trust me, have no reason. If I knew then what I know now, I wouldn't have worried about anything."

Eleanor stood, replaced the towels on the chair, pulled up the window blinds. She tried to slide the glass up, but it wouldn't move.

"They don't let you open the windows?"

"Nuh. Thing. At. All to be stressed about!"

"People don't just stress over nothing," Eleanor raised her voice. "That doesn't even make sense. If I'm stressed there's probably a reason for it. There are reasons people get stressed."

"You have it easy. You're lucky. When I was your age, think of it, evacuating Kaiserwald, walking along those terrible train tracks. The Nazis firing at us. Starving us. We walked naked! They had us all marching completely naked, four-by-four like a pack of animals."

Mary began to twitch. Eleanor picked up a watch from the table and wove it around her fingers.

"Mom."

"Marching four-by-four. Without shoes. Barefoot. Stripped bare. You don't know humiliation like that. You have something to stress about?"

"Please, just stop."

"You're lucky I survived to have you."

Eleanor put down the watch and faced her mother. "You weren't at Kaiserwald. You weren't even alive yet. You're not from Europe. You've never even been to Germany, or Latvia once in your life. You've never even left North America."

"But you learn to adjust. Amazing, the will to survive. It's supernatural, really."

Eleanor opened her purse, rifled for her keys. "I need to leave."

"Already? Oh. You just got here."

"I've been here a while. I have to go to work."

"Can I have a hug before you go?"

Eleanor did not want to hug her mother, but she placed her arms lightly around her.

Mary whispered, "Are you still doing that thing?"

"I told you I wasn't."

"I don't want you doing that thing."

Nicholas arrived home late, clearly exhausted from a day of sales-pitching unemployed Bhutanese and Iraqi refugees to dismissive businessmen, grocery store owners, fast-food chain managers. To Laundromat owners. To convenience store clerks. He had spent the day driving his beat-up Volkswagen around the city, insisting that refugees were hard workers, that they wanted to be in America, so they would care about their work. He explained to the employers that many of his refugees had earned advanced degrees in their home nations. He sweat and stuttered. In between, he made home visits to the refugees' apartments.

"You should see the shit holes we find them," Nicholas said. He hunched forward on his parents' couch, pulled off his shoes and socks with effort. "The cheapest places in the city. Roach infested, moldy, disgusting. There's usually like ten of them living in a one-bedroom. Whole families. It's not right. They shouldn't have to live like that."

Eleanor sat beside him. She kissed him three times. She thought this was the right amount.

Dawn sat on another couch, across from them. She had the television on, and was working on her laptop. Eleanor thought Dawn's dyed black and permed hair looked fried. Her bangs were cut at a severe, odd angle across her forehead. She wore fake nails, and gaudy mix of plastic jewelry. Nicholas had once told Eleanor that his mother, a real estate agent, prided herself on looking young. Eleanor could sense herself judging Dawn, which made her feel ashamed of herself.

"We stock their kitchens," Nicholas went on, "but sometimes they don't know what to do with the kinds of food we buy. Chips and two-liters of soda. We should be buying fresh produce, food they know. One of my coworkers found a family sitting around a fire they made in their living room. They caught a squirrel and were cooking it."

Eleanor put her hand on Nicholas' thigh and thought about making him feel good that night. She thought about what she might do. She would pull off his clothes, kiss his neck, his collarbone, his nipples, she would wrap her hands around his cock. She didn't want to forget the way she had felt in the car. She wanted to follow through.

In the kitchen, Martin was preparing dinner. Burgers and rice pilaf. Nicholas fell asleep on the couch. Dawn tapped at her keyboard, now and then, looking up at the television, laughing. Once or twice, she rewound the show, then called for Martin. "You have to see this," she said. "Look, look!"

When dinner was nearly ready, Eleanor microwaved a veggie burger for herself. They thought she was a vegetarian, and usually she was. She could choose not to eat Martin's rice or burgers. It was important to be able to choose. She helped Martin set the table, brought food into the dining room. In the room, framed photographs of Martin's side of the family hung on the walls, generations gathered for holidays and reunions. There was a portrait of Martin, Dawn and Nicholas posed in a beige Sears studio, and portrait of a dog and a cat, two pets that were now dead, sitting tensely side by side.

"I'm sorry you don't like your job, honey," Dawn said to Nicholas, when they were seated at the table.

"These people are just so frustrating. They say, 'Why would I want to hire immigrants who can't even speak English in this economy? People born in America can't even get work.' They think the Bhutanese are Muslim, and they don't want to hire Muslims."

"That's terrible, honey. People can be cruel. I've been working with this adorable young couple, just married, buying their first house. I brought them for what was supposed to be their final walk-through this morning. Oh, they were so excited. But when we got there we found the place smashed to bits. Walls beat in, banisters snapped. Staircases totally destroyed. Windows broken. The former owner, the man who lost the place, did it all. He took a hammer and demolished the garage. Oh my lord. It's such a mess."

"This one refugee, Ram. He's got one long thumbnail." Nicholas held a finger two inches away from the top of his thumb. "That long, and curling. I tell him he has to cut it if he's going to get a job and he says, 'I'm waiting to cut it until I get a job. For good luck!' I'm like, 'No, you have to cut it now.'"

"All the wires were pulled out of the place too. I thought, not again. It wasn't the first time this guy came back to make trouble. He thinks if he can't live in the house, no one should.

"You know what I found in the storage space? Your old Ninja Turtles figurines. You used to love the Ninja Turtles. Remember when we used to watch the show together? You'd watch it while I folded laundry. You sat in the laundry basket. We still have the same one. 'Teenage mutant ninja turtles. Teenage mutant ninja turtles. Heroes in a half-shell! Turtle power!'"

As Nicholas and his mother went on, Eleanor studied the photographs on the wall. She thought she might want to eat the rice, but she did not eat any rice.

After dinner she went to the basement while Martin and Nicholas played instruments together upstairs, Martin on his keyboard, Nicholas on his guitar. The music mingled with the sounds from Dawn's television. Eleanor tried to get some work done. She was behind on her stories. She typed a couple sloppy sentences about the selectman's meeting. She tried to make sense of her notes. She thought about finally being one to instigate sex. She thought about Nicholas coming downstairs, seeing an eager look come across his face when he found her there, waiting for him, perhaps naked.

The music stopped and Nicholas came downstairs. He went immediately into the bathroom, and she heard him brush his teeth, floss. He came out yawning. He sat on the bed, squirmed out of his clothes. His legs were thin and pale. Eleanor sat beside him. He turned on the nightstand lamp and got out his book. She got out her book and lay next to him and stared at a page, read the same line five, six times. When she looked at Nicholas, he had fallen asleep.

Eleanor watched him. She stared at the ceiling, and out the pointless basement window. She looked at Nicholas, out the window, at the dark wall. She waited for Nicholas to reach for her, to scrape his fingers across her stomach, to move them lower. She heard his breathing shift into a low, deep sleep.

She slipped her hand beneath the elastic band of her sweatpants, and then the band of her underwear. She crawled her fingers through the small hairs and worked them there, untangling the hairs, pulling them straight and letting them settle back down. She slipped her fingers lower. She closed her eyes and tried to think up the men she sometimes imagined when she was alone, the rough men who swore and pulled girl's hair, who knew how to turn a girl into nothing, and take away all of her responsibility. Lying next to Nicholas, the private men could not work.

She did not want to resort to tiptoeing upstairs, to the small liquor cabinet. Taking Dawn and Martin's alcohol made her feel like a drunk and a freeloader. She did not want to risk waking anyone by unlocking the back door to smoke a cigarette in the dew and moonlight of the back porch. It was likely she was hungry, but if she ate even a bite of an apple, she might not be able to stop. She might empty out the kitchen, then the cupboards, then the city, the state. She might eat up the world. She told herself to stay where she was, focus on her breathing, to understand that there was nothing she could do. Why bother, she thought. She thought it until she felt as though there wasn't anything important in the world, nothing to have and nothing to want.

She woke with a vague sense of anger. She found a note on the nightstand:

Be Good! Love N.

Eleanor left the note on the table. She dressed and left the house. At the gas station down the road she bought a dusty bottle of wine. She uncorked it in the basement, drank it from a mug, waited for Alec's wife's Mercedes. Upstairs, Martin worked in his office.

The office's window faced the road, and she did not want Martin to see the car pull up. She drank the wine quickly, two small pours, and let herself begin to feel warm and more relaxed. What did Nicholas know about being good? What did good behavior have to do with feeling good?

When the Mercedes pulled into the driveway, Eleanor thought: stay in the car. Alec stepped out of the car and stretched his body. Eleanor pulled on a sweater, found her purse, shoved her feet into her shoes and found herself standing in front of him. She did not give him time to ring the doorbell. Alec wore shiny leather loafers, a pressed shirt tucked into pressed slacks.

"Hi kiddo," he said. "Good to see you."

He opened his arms and she hugged him quickly. He opened her door. She presented a closed-mouth smile, one that she thought was the right smile. The car smelled of leather, of burl wood, of coffee. She could have offered to meet him at the restaurant. Would that have been more appropriate? He pulled onto the highway and headed east down Route 101.

"What do you think of the car?" he asked.

"It's nice. It's bigger than I thought it would be."

"That's real wood trim." He ran his hand over the dash. "Was that your house?"

Eleanor sometimes had trouble mentioning Nicholas

to other men. She did not want to upset them. Men were fragile, overt about their fragility, obvious in their disappointment. So dismissive when they received the smallest unintended blow. But she wanted to practice honesty. Maybe Alec would surprise her.

"I'm staying with my boyfriend's parents right now."

"Oh. Great," Alec said. He gazed at her quickly, then into the rearview mirror. "What does your boyfriend do?"

"He resettles refugees. Mostly Bhutanese, but some Iraqis. He's an employment counselor. Helps them find jobs."

"Resettles refugees, huh." Alec paused. "That's really something. That's commendable. He must be a really great guy."

"He is. It's difficult though, finding refugees jobs."

"I'd imagine most folks don't trust Muslims right now. I can see it being difficult."

Eleanor asked Alec questions about himself. His job, his childhood. He was retired. He owned beach vacation properties that he spruced up and rented out in the summer. They dotted the streets of Hampton Beach, not far from the seaside restaurant where they would have lunch. He talked about his wife, the teacher. He told a story about growing up in the woods of Northern Canada, scouring the forests for spirits and hunting, being a boy.

"I had a guru. An old Aboriginal man who lived in

the woods and didn't tell you anything. You just had to follow him if you wanted to learn," he said.

Alec had run for the selectman position because he had too much time on his hands.

"I wanted to give back to the community. I'm doing the job, but only for one term. I won't run again. Someone else ought to step in and do their civic duty. I'm not like Harvey or Heather, those old windbags. They'll be selectmen until they die. No, I won't run again."

Eleanor looked at the trees whirring by, at Alec, down to her knees. She looked at each of these the appropriate amount of times. She sat appropriately straight. She crossed her legs at the ankle. She liked the blur of landscape, the way everything else seemed to be moving while she stayed still.

"When I was consulting," Alec said, "I tell you, I traveled just all over, across the globe to transform these mammoth corporations, make them efficient. In Japan it was always a whirlwind. They would usher me into a car the second I stepped off the plane and swoop me off to the hotel where the employees teared up if you didn't let them do their jobs. The elevator man teared up if I didn't let him push the elevator button. The room attendant cried if I didn't let him turn on the showerhead. It was just surreal. I thought about moving there but despite the culture, despite the beautiful women everywhere, it was just too different, especially the divide between the treatment of men and women."

"I can imagine," Eleanor said.

"I was hoping you could be my niece. I could do nice things for you, take you shopping."

"Don't you have any nieces?" Eleanor asked.

By the time they reached Sanders Restaurant, thick rolls of clouds blanketed the sky. Alec opened Eleanor's car door. The dining room of the restaurant was lit by sunlight, wood-paneled, and nautical-themed. Eleanor half-expected a fat fiddle player to jump through the kitchen door.

"Where would you like to sit?" Alec asked.

Eleanor scanned the wide room. Windows overlooked the water. A mahogany bar lined one wall. Two middle-aged women with outdated, feathered hair, and eccentric jewelry, gossiped on bar stools. Otherwise the room was empty.

"We can sit here in the bar, or in the nice sunny porch room, just over there." Alec pointed to a hallway.

Eleanor did not know what to say. "I'd be fine wherever."

"Let's go into the porch room. It's less stuffy in there."

"Okay," she said.

A waitress seated them by the long row of windows. Alec suggested Eleanor try the signature martini. He ordered a black and tan for himself. He ordered the appetizer platter of crab cakes, shrimp cocktail, bruschetta, bacon-wrapped scallops, and baked bread.

The buzz of the morning wine had begun to dwindle into lethargy, and the martini felt good.

"On the scale of one to ten, you are an eleven," Alec said.

The waitress brought the appetizer platter.

"You are the kind of girl who eats?" Alec asked.

"I eat. I eat a lot."

"Good. You're so thin. I can never tell."

It clouded over and began to drizzle. The harbor's sailboats and yachts rocked on their moorings. Alec cut the crab cake and slid half onto Eleanor's plate. She ate the crab cake. She ate shrimp cocktail and a scallop. Alec took small, deliberate bites and chewed slowly, rolling the flavors over his tongue. When the waitress came with another round drinks, she smiled and Eleanor thought she must have been constructing an embarrassing narrative of the two of them.

The crab cake and the shrimp, the scallop, and bruschetta felt heavy in her stomach. She felt the food pressing back up, tight like a bear hug from inside her gut. Their entrées came. Eleanor ate her pasta in large bites. She chewed quickly and followed each bite with another.

Alec pointed out the window. "See that?" A tethered sailboat. "I'd like a boat like that. A beautiful seventeen-foot sailboat with a cabin large enough for a bed and a deck big enough to lie out on. No speedboat for me. I just want a nice leisure cruise." He reclined and clasped his hands in his lap. "I'd go everywhere."

Eleanor imagined Alec with a young woman. She in a string bikini, and Alec dressed in airy slacks, an expensive linen shirt. She saw him on a picnic blanket with the women, Alec pulling her close with one arm. Then, Alec's eyes and lips surprised Eleanor by turning sad, almost mournful.

"You know," he said, "you really don't know what this means to me, you coming out here. I spend so much time by myself. I'm always by myself. This has really been the best day I've had in a very long time." He pressed his lips together and tried to smile, but he only managed an achy, distorted frown. He looked sad and vulnerable, as though Eleanor could hurt him.

"Sorry," he said. "I'm just happy."

They left Sanders Restaurant and drove south towards Hampton Beach. In the summer months, this was the most crowded part of the state's meager coastline. It grew thick with teenagers following each other like puppies. But it was off-season and boards covered the souvenir shops, fried dough stands, arcades. A few lonely tourists huddled under dripping awnings.

"Why don't I show you one of my rental properties," Alec said. "I'd love to show you how I decorate them, while we're in the area."

Her stomach felt burned from the meal, and she felt uneasy about the proposal. She thought she should tell him she needed to go home, but she just said, "That'd be nice."

"Why don't I reserve a weekend this summer for you and your boyfriend? There are still quite a few weekends open."

"That would be really great, actually."

"You and your boyfriend can have a nice vacation."

"We could definitely use a vacation."

They arrived at a small cottage with a white picket fence and a clean slatted porch. Alec checked the mail and spoke briefly with a neighbor before he led Eleanor up a set of stairs, opened the door, and directed her into the kitchen.

"This is it," he said. He spread his arms in a show. He opened up the cupboards to illustrate how he took care of his guests, stocked his properties with food.

"I keep Goldfish and fruit snacks for the kids. Liquor and beer in the fridge, too. I tell them, 'Use anything you want.'"

He toured her through the small, typical beachside apartment. Two bedrooms. In one, bunk beds against the wall, paintings of coastal landscapes. Shelves displayed conch shells and model boats. Eleanor tried not appear anxious about being in Alec's guest house or being in pain. Acid tore at her throat.

Alec reached for a bottle of vodka from one of the shelves. "Shall we have a drink before getting on the road?"

Nothing can ever just be nice and stay nice, Eleanor thought.

"I should be getting home," she said.

"We could just have one drink," he said. Then, "It's all right. I understand."

She gave him an appropriate smile, and felt relieved.

"Come here," he said. He tugged Eleanor by the waist, pressed her body into his chest. He anchored one hand on her shoulder and another on her waist. She shut her eyes and froze. He lowered his head and when he kissed her cheek his eyelashes brushed her face. She sucked in her gut so Alec wouldn't have to feel her bloated stomach.

"An uncle can kiss his niece," he said. "An uncle can do that."

Eleanor searched the room but she did not know what she was looking for. She settled on the clean linoleum floor. Alec hooked his fingers around her jaw and wrenched her face towards his.

He said she had lovely hair, asked Eleanor if he could touch it. She did not tell him no. They drove northwest, back towards the city.

"There are some nice outlets across the bridge in Kittery. Do you like to go shopping? I was thinking I could take you there sometime," he said.

Then they drove in silence. Eleanor looked out the window, but she didn't see anything and her mind felt blank. Alec coughed a few times. Nearing Nicholas' parents' house, he turned to her.

"You have a boyfriend? You have a boyfriend. I suppose this can't work, can it?"

"I don't think so," Eleanor said.

"Okay, kiddo. No hard feelings."

In the driveway of Nicholas's parents' house, they shook hands and he pulled the Mercedes into the road. She went in through the garage. She could hear jazz music and unfamiliar voices coming from the first floor. She took a deep breath and headed towards the noises.

In the living room, Bhutanese refugees sat reclined on the sofas and chairs pulled from the dining room. Women dressed in colorful clothes. They had dots in the middle of their foreheads and sat quietly, smiling, observing their children. Young men with bare feet and white shirts crossed their legs at the ankles. Two silent children stretched out upside-down in one woman's lap. The children flipped around and sat up, pressed their faces into their mothers' bodies.

Nicholas sat sandwiched between two of the men on the couch. He put the half-eaten plate of food on the table and met Eleanor at the stairs.

"Hi. How was your day?" He touched her arm and Eleanor produced a smile. He seemed more awake than he had in days. "These are my friends, some of the refugees I've been helping. Everybody, this is Eleanor."

They lined up to shake her hand, and Nicholas recited his guests' names.

"This is Deepak, Pema, Bibek. Purna, Tika. This is Ram."

She took Ram's hand and glanced down at his fingers. He must have cut off his one long nail. She wondered if that meant he got a job. The coffee table was covered by half-eaten plates of hot food: lentils and rice, flat breads, curried chicken. More women in the kitchen chatted as they fried and boiled more food.

"Have a seat," Nicholas said. "They wanted to cook for us."

A woman entered from the kitchen with a plate and handed it to Eleanor. Eleanor thanked her, sat, took a bite. She watched the refugees watch her eat. The food was rich and hearty, home-cooked and perfect, but she felt nauseous. The group studied her face as she brought her fork to her mouth.

"Delicious," she said.

"Mr. Nicholas," Ram said, "You think we may find work?"

Nicholas returned to the seat the refugees were saving for him. "Well, there may be some new openings at a supermarket downtown. You could work in produce. Do you like produce? Vegetables?" Nicholas said.

"Yes," Ram said, "Very much."

The women fed the children. They talked to each other in Nepali and laughed often. When plates were empty, the women refilled them, bringing out more hot curries and samosas.

"It's very good," Eleanor said to a woman standing next to her, watching her eat.

The men were saying to her, "Mr. Nicholas is so good a man. Mr. Nicholas. A very good friend."

Eleanor stood and thanked the refugees for the meal.

She walked to Nicholas and whispered she was going downstairs.

"Is everything okay?" Nicholas asked.

"Everything's fine," she said. "I'm just tired."

"It was a long day." He kissed her forehead.

She passed the basement bathroom and went into the bedroom. She pulled off her pants in the dark. She lowered herself onto the bed and clutched her belly, then lay very still and did not pull up the covers over her body. The noise persisted above her. She swallowed food that pushed into her mouth. Her throat burned and her stomach ached. She lay in bed and dug her head into the pillow and fell asleep.

When she woke Nicholas lay next to her, on his back. She lifted herself out of bed and slid her hand along the wall to find the bathroom. She closed the door, turned on the light, the fan. She pulled off her shirt so she wouldn't dirty its collar, moved the rug out from around the toilet and put up the seat. She took a deep breath and contracted her stomach, to push its contents up and up against her throat. She slid two fingers into her mouth, past her teeth, past the ridges of her hard palate, between her tonsils. She heard Mary's voice floating above her, are you still doing that thing? "No," she said. "Stop." She removed her fingers from her mouth, squeezed her eyes shut and let out a deep, helpless moan. She turned off the fan and the light, and found her way back to the bed.

Eleanor woke, tangled in damp clothes and sheets. She sat up, found the shape of Nicholas lying next to her. Her phone beeped, and she reached for it. The text message from Alec read: Still friends?

Nicholas began to stir. He shifted and pressed his eyelids closed until they flittered open. He looked confused in the mornings. She touched his arm. She smiled at him a little, and he smiled back.

"Who was that?" Nicholas asked.

"No one," she said. "How did you sleep?"

"Fine."

Nicholas looked happy, relaxed, not as stressed as he usually did waking up. Perhaps it was the result of the refugees' visit, their show of thanks. He lifted his body onto his elbows, kissed her on the cheeks, then the lips. Eleanor watched his hand move under the covers, felt it touch her leg. He kissed her again. His hands crept to her thigh. She stopped it with her hand and looked at him.

"I have something to tell you," she said. "It's about yesterday. Something happened with Alec."

"What happened?"

"He tried to kiss me. He did kiss me. I didn't want him to."

"I'm sorry," he said. "Is that all that happened?"

No, she thought. She looked him in the eyes and said, "No."

Then she told him about the rape.

III

THE TROUBLE WITH LANGUAGE

L ast night I went to bed thinking that old, endless, quiet thought: I don't want to ever die.

Then, in the deep of night my husband shuddered a little, put his hand on my arm, bolted onto his elbow and looked at me. It was dark. I could only see the shape of him. He said with strange conviction, "I love you."

He said it like he had just remembered how deeply he could love. Like he had just discovered what love is really. I kissed him on his forehead, then his shoulder. I thought he must be feeling something important.

The final dream I had last night was about my mother. I bumped into her at the grocery store deli counter. She was trying desperately to place her order, stuttering her words. On the other side of the counter two middle-aged women clad in hairnets and aprons did a mocking, eye rolling thing.

"I don't know. I'll take. Wait. I don't know," my

mother said. She did not know what she wanted to say, or she did not know how to say it.

One of the women scowled and said, "You're giving us a lesson in patience and endurance."

"Yes," my mother said, and looked at the floor. She walked away with nothing. It seemed to me that the trouble was not my mother's lack of language, but the women's lack of compassion.

When I woke, it was summer in the north. The sun lit the sky softly like a film of jelly over dark toast, orange in the underbelly of the clouds. All was very quiet except the cat. I fed him and then let him out the back door. He stood on the rusty fire escape, mewed into the sky, and woke my husband.

My husband walked through the kitchen, slow and heavy-lidded. "Come on," he said to the cat, and carried it back to bed. There weren't any dreams or mewing after that. Just a sleeping man and a sleeping cat. The apartment grew still and strange and empty.

RAPID SHRINKING

A group of elderly people sat around a table in a chain coffee shop. They didn't mind just sitting and talking. They probably came there every day. They did not want to speak overtly about their own failing bodies, but one old woman told the others about someone who was hit by a subway train, and lost both her legs.

The story of the legless woman made the news. The elderly lady was talking and wondering how it all had happened. Did the woman jump or did she fall? Was she pushed?

One elderly man said, "It's okay, they make good prosthetics these days."

Another said "I would rather be dead than have no legs."

"What's saddest of all," said the elderly women, "is this is the last we will hear about her in the news. The reporters will have all moved on."

I had been experiencing rapid shrinking all week.

I was shrinking from the inside out—bones, muscles, nerves, then organs. My insides shrank first and then my skin imploded around a tiny version of myself. For a minute or two, before my hair shrunk down, I felt, almost, like air.

I was embarrassed about the whole occurrence, so I temporarily moved out of the house. I told my husband I needed to buy some milk, checked into a cheap hotel. I did not answer my phone when my husband called. I would make up some story when I returned home. I was kidnapped. I was lost. I was flying.

In the hotel room, I started making white paper cranes to keep my mind off the shrinking. I sat cross-legged on the bed, worked until the paper cranes, the size of flies, covered the comforter, then the floor, then the television and set of matching chairs. It was nice to increase the volume of something for once for once for once. A fire alarm went off, but I thought I must be dreaming. Those cranes on the radiator are not ablaze. I was never any larger than I am.

GETTING OUT OF THIS HOUSE

I keep telling myself I could get out of my house by going straight, but I keep finding myself deeper into all the rooms. I'm not even sure it's my house anymore. I never would have chosen seafoam green for the walls. I never would have upholstered a couch with seventeenth-century velvet. And I keep meeting people I've never seen before. Someone who calls herself my aunt walks around naked and drinks lemon ginger tea. Someone who calls herself my sister is holding a gun.

Letters keep coming for people who do not live here. Who do not live here anymore or haven't yet arrived. I like seeing these thin packages slip through the mail slot. They remind me that I'm only a pit stop here, a temporary invasion.

Today, somebody delivered an arrest warrant for a person I've never met. Chances are, he is long gone. Still, I called the number and turned myself in, waited for the cruiser to take me away. I wanted so bad to get out of this house.

At the police station, an officer asked me questions about my comprehension of the law, about my mental state, about my name. I answered the best I could, considering all the facts I did not know. He asked me, "Do you understand your crime?" He said the laws are the laws for a reason. I thought about all the crimes I had committed, but had gotten away with. I thought about all the actions I had taken that were innocent but punished.

In the holding cell, a man looked at me and said he did not do it. He said, "I know you." Then, "On second thought, I don't."

When the guard came back, I was free to go. He led me out of the station, warned me not to confuse myself with other people, handed me the business card of a local psychoanalyst. But the address on the card was my own address. How did I end up back in this house? How did I ever leave?

OUTSIDE AND INSIDE

It wasn't like this yesterday. The bears stare into everybody's windows, their paws making cups between little black eyes and reflective glass. Other things that have changed: There aren't any explanations left. No bridges from Alaska to Russia. No tiny volcanoes of blame. Do you know how empathy works? We don't love what we don't know. We don't cry for a tragedy we don't see. We don't feel bayonets sticking somebody else's skin. We don't drown ourselves in oceans that exist on other planets.

The grizzly bears don't want to bother us. They just want to look in and make us wonder whether or not they are our friends. I don't know if I've loved a lot of bears, but when I was a girl, my best friend ripped her hair from her scalp, told me it didn't hurt. I crushed bees in my palms and wiped the paste on the roof of my mouth. I screwed in all the light bulbs I could find, then closed my eyes.

Up in the attic, I chip tiny holes into the roof. I imagine the possibility of an entire sky. Downstairs, my child, who once screamed and covered her ears during fireworks, now crawls up to the bears and puts her pink hands to the glass. She laughs and pets like a lover before the truth. She doesn't know about bears, and I don't try to explain. Whatever the bears have planned for me, they also have planned for her.

At night, rain falls through the roof's holes. For a moment, we believe we are putting out a fire in another part of town.

YES AND NO

When I am asked if I am getting better my reply should be "No" because my symptoms have not changed. But when somebody asks me this question, they often offer such a look of concern or hope that I am compelled to answer "Yes" instead. After I say "Yes" the person perks up so quickly with relief. She is able to continue on to the grocery store, or the zoo, or the bar without distress. So I think, even if I am not getting any better, at least I have helped someone else feel better. Making other people feel better often makes me feel better, in which case, by answering "Yes" even though my illness has not actually changed, I do, in a sense, feel better.

If I answer "Yes" however, when the truth is "No," I cannot help but wonder about all those times I may have been deceived by the responses of others, when I have asked if they are feeling better. If I learned, for instance, that Sally, who has for some time been suffering seizures and dizzy spells, had been telling me "Yes" when the truth was "No," I would surely feel worse.

If Sally had told me she was not feeling better, perhaps I could have offered my assistance. I could have cooked her a chicken dinner or picked up her children from their after-school program. I could have mowed her lawn or bent down to fetch her car keys when she dropped them. Then, Sally would have enjoyed some much-needed rest, and I would have felt better for helping. I have to wonder, might the people who ask me, "Are you getting better?" prefer I say "No" so they can help me and feel good?

If I answer "No," and then you ask me how you can help, I may be inclined to say, "I would love for you to hug me right now, and allow me to burrow my nose in the shoulder of your warm, black coat, at least until this street I have been walking for so long, so long, stops stretching and jiggling like an elastic band, miles and miles in either direction." As I walk, I hear a jingling. It feels as though someone is throwing change at my heels. I can almost feel a phantom's breath in my back as he throws pennies at my feet. Though, I cannot see him, no I can't. Not as I see the groups of strange children huddling in the trees by my mother's home, where I live in the basement. They are chanting round a fire, while I am so alone. Oh, I would love for you to open your arms and embrace me tightly so we could both experience a yes-calm that accompanies human contact.

There is, of course, the possibility I am not feeling better, but alas, I am not in any danger either. At least I don't think I am in any immediate danger. My illness is simply something I must learn to live with. Besides, in all honesty, how much can someone who knows nothing about schizophrenia actually help?

People tend to overreact, don't they, when you tell them you are feeling worse. "Oh, I'm so sorry. What can I do? I shall pace my bedroom through the night worrying and wondering how you are getting on! Oh, darling, is there a doctor I can call?"

I might become obliged to deal with, on top of my own illness, the burden of other people's fear. I may as well answer "Yes" even though the proper answer is "No."

While getting worse may be a terrifying thought, so is returning to a healthy old ordinary. Oh, an ordinary, hum-drum life! How could I manage to live with that, now that the roads have come alive just for me? And sometimes the morning sparrows speak me all their woes, so pleased they are that a more evolved life form has taken an interest in them.

"And are you feeling better?" I ask the birds. "It is

difficult," they say, "to hoist one's body to the air, with so few opportunities for worms nowadays."

The birds sing and do not judge, not like a human being would. If I said, "Sally, I am worse, and here's why," do you think she would feel comfortable, later, discussing her problems with me? "No way I want you to make me a chicken dinner," she might say. "Not you, nutsy. You freak. I don't want you anywhere near my kids."

And then, I would feel much worse.

Another possibility: I am not schizophrenic at all, but sociopathic, as the doctors say. I have been inventing my sickness to amuse myself at the expense of the likes of you. What do you think of that? Fooled you. But then, I fooled me too.

In the case I am a sociopath, I am likely not improving, but also not getting much worse, and perhaps I ought to be asked a different question from the start. Or told, instead of asked at all.

Perhaps the reason I would not be told: There is something naturally sociopathic about this business of answering a simple question of yes and no. Still, it is better than being asked no question at all. Yes, it is better than that.

A FAILED KIDNAPPING

I would like to kidnap my childhood friend, Demitra. This will not be easy to do. I have not seen or heard from Demitra in twelve long years and, though I think I have seen her on the Psychic Network, I do not know where she is. She could be on top of a mountain, or swimming in a pool, or shaving her armpits over a sink.

I am lying in bed, wondering where to start. My husband is awake now, getting ready for the day, but I am afraid to get out of bed. I do not like days very much anymore. Days are like snakes. They tempt me to do complicated things. I hear water boiling for the French press, and my husband dropping a bagel into the toaster. I pull the covers over my head.

Demitra is a psychic. This much I know. I close my eyes tightly and try to speak to her with my mind. "Demitra, please let me know where you are. I remember your golden hair and your big, sad eyes. I want to kidnap you, if it comes to that."

I think about all the dead people I have ever known. My mother's father and my father's mother are sitting on the couch of my childhood house, blinking and looking at each other.

"Who the hell are you?" my grandmother asks.

"I don't know," says my grandfather. "Could be I'm dead."

My grandmother is holding a paper bag of plastic toys that she has collected from cereal boxes and home shopping channels. She is frowning, but I love gifts! When I go to retrieve a toy from the bag, she slaps my hand. "That's not for you," she says. "You were always such a greedy child."

My grandfather is holding a pencil and a pad of paper. He asks me to come sit next to him and draw. I sit next to him and he gives me a piece of paper, snaps the pencil in half, and sharpens it for me. A tree sprouts in front of us and we draw the tree in silence. After a half hour, I look at his paper, but it is blank.

"I need your help," I say to the dead grandparents.

"Humph," my grandmother says, "Nobody ever helped me!"

My grandfather only looks at me dumbly.

"It's okay," I say to the two dead grandparents. "You can go."

They both disappear.

My husband lies on me on the bed, shiny eyes and mouth with smile. "Morning!" he says, and shakes me. Words are streaming out of his mouth. I try very hard to listen and understand.

He is in bed now, and I am standing up. I am pacing around the apartment feeling for ghosts. Our cat follows me around. I pet the cat and think, if I do not do anything else in my life but take care of this little gray cat, if I do not go outside and just stay here and be nice to a cat, I would not have caused any trouble for the rest of my days, and maybe I will feel okay when I die.

"That's no way to think," says my husband. I smile. He hands me a cup of coffee. Outside, it's raining and gray. My cat rubs his head on my leg.

"I want to find my old best friend, Demitra," I say, "I am going to kidnap her and make her find the ghost in the house."

"You'll have to go outside for that," my lover says, and I know he is probably right.

It takes me four hours to go outside. I watch a lot of TV and I eat two slices of maple sugar pie. I feel sugar-sick. I try to sleep. My head is on a lazy Susan. A voice inside my head says, "Gross."

You are right, voice, I think, you are right. I roll up my sleeve and scrub dried food off the dishes. Ketchup flecks and chicken bits circle the drain. I soak myself down in the shower. I rub the soap on a washcloth and rub the washcloth on my skin. Scrubbing feels good. I am ready to go out.

What will I ask Demitra after I have kidnapped her? Does she remember the first time we played in second grade? I helped her find the alphabet letters that Ted wrote for her in the clouds. Ted was Demitra's first best friend. His appendix burst and he died. When I found a letter I checked with Demitra to make sure I had seen things right. "Is that an A?" I would ask, and she would say, "Write it down!" Then, Demitra unscrambled the letters into words, like "chilly" and "rascal" and "long." She grinned for a while, but I worried I hadn't really spotted any letters at all. I had only been making them up because I wanted to play.

The world is so big. It stretches forever in all directions, goes on and on. I walk up a hill and look at the faces of walking people. Some of them smile and some of them frown. I worry I am frowning, and try to smile. I make eye contact, and then look away when eye contact is returned.

I make eye contact with a little girl through the glass of a coffee shop window. I enter, order an espresso and think about Demitra. Did she believe we were witches, back in fourth grade, when we stood in a circle in the park, held knives to each other's throats, recited initiation incantations, and became an official coven?

The little girl draws a picture next to me. She shows me her picture of a monster riding a unicorn.

"That's a good picture," I say, and she says it's lousy.

"The monster is too lumpy, and the unicorn's a unicow. Besides, it's all I can ever think to draw. Would you tell me a story, or what?"

Once upon a time a girl had a best friend named Demitra. Demitra was a psychic, but nobody believed her. Not even the girl, not really. To cope with her loneliness, Demitra cut her skin and pulled out her hair. Demitra smiled as she pulled out her hair in front of the girl, and said, "See, it doesn't hurt." Her best friend did not know what to believe, the smile, or her understanding of pain. One day Demitra took a whole bottle of aspirin. Alas, she did not die.

The little girl says, "That's a very sad story," and I say it is, but it has a happy ending.

One day, Demitra decided, "I am a psychic and that's the way it is." She moved to a farmhouse and opened a psychic studio. To this day she has exorcized eighty-three trapped souls and helped forty-eight pet owners speak to their pets. She lived happily ever after, and that's the end.

The little girl crumples up her drawing and tells me she has a secret. She has a very big secret and she is going to tell me now. The little girl says she is not a little girl at all but a moose. She is finally ready to commit to being a moose.

We walk to a nearby park and stand in the middle of a lot of grass. The little girl asks me to hold her hand because she is nervous about transforming into a moose. Small tears form in her eyes and I wipe them away with a tissue.

"Okay?" I say.

"Okay."

I watch the little girl become a moose. It takes some time. At first, she looks like she's constipated; her insides vibrate underneath her skin. She lets out a couple little yelps. Her body bulges and her eyes bug out. Antlers brake through her forehead and she grows very large. Finally, she is a completely grand, majestic moose. She grunts at me and says she will miss some things about her human form. Eating chocolate, for example, and jumping rope. She bares her teeth and thumps away towards a section of the park that is layered with trees.

Back home, I wait for my husband to return from work. I fry a cheese sandwich and microwave tomato soup. I sit on the couch and look around the house. It feels very small and very large, like a cage with no walls. A book falls off the bookshelf, so I pick it up and read. The book is about a man who had killed another man, but can't remember that he did. When my husband comes home, we kiss. I look out the window and we hug.

"Did you find Demitra?" he asks.

I say I did not get the chance to start looking.

We watch TV in bed, to fall asleep. We complain about TV, but lately we have been watching a lot. We watch a TV show about a man who has killed a man and remembers it, and is in trouble with the law.

After the show, my husband says, "I hate TV. A show starts good, and then it just gets worse and worse, like the creators don't have a clue. But the suspense makes me want to keep watching." I pull the covers up to my ears and blink and think: like life.

Sometimes I talk to my husband without speaking. I say, "I love you so much. I love you more than the sun. I want to crawl into your body and fill you up." I wait for him to smile, or blush, to say something back, using his mouth, or not.

You can try not to blame him for your lack of communication. You can believe he reciprocates, anyway, even if you aren't sure. You can tell yourself loving is better than being loved, and even though he doesn't hear it, it doesn't mean it isn't true.

The cat attacks my leg. His ears shoot back and his eyes are nuts. When I say, "Stop, cat," he walks a circle around himself, settles down and licks his leg.

Maybe tomorrow, I think, as I lay on my back, in bed. But before I can think about what might happen tomorrow, what I might do, or whether or not I will believe, I am not here anymore. I do not know where I am. I am someplace else entirely.

THE OPPOSITE OF ENTROPY

My father says consciousness is the opposite of entropy. But entropy is so strong that I let the morning's extra coffee sit in the pot all day. I drank so much coffee that all I could do was run. I ran every day for fifty-seven years. I passed a dead raccoon decomposing by the side of the road.

The raccoon was my friend. My heart rate rose each time I approached the spot where his body slowly changed. Anticipation makes my stomach explode, like waking up from a dream. It's almost too much.

But I compensate. I balance. Yesterday I told myself that I don't have to do anything. I lay in bed and stared at a blank wall for two hours, the safest thing I did all week. I felt my soul rise out of my body like a hot-air balloon captained by a pirate.

When my soul returned, the pirate told me that the world outside had changed. A beautiful giantess walked the streets, touching her soft hands to the tops of buildings like a saint. Nobody slept as she walked. They lay in bed, barely breathing, waiting for the giantess to disappear. Nobody knows what do to with such a massive beauty.

My husband says the more you know, the stupider you become. The less capable of making any decision at all. We were driving to the ocean and I wanted to kiss him, or anybody so long as the kiss was shared. I wanted to feel as I did when I was staring at a wall.

When we got home a homeless man was lying on our porch, waiting for my inability to say no. I had made a habit of giving him rations of cigarette, tea bags. I couldn't, so my husband asked the man to leave for me. Please don't come back, he said. You are taking advantage of her kindness.

GOING TO THE DINER

I have left a man in bed with the idea of myself. Without him, I wander through the town. Everyone is sleeping or else dancing where the forest meets the street.

Here, the drunks are singing their songs, bonding over let's not change tonight. I watch them like a photographer watches the slow twitch of her subject. There, a line of blind girls, single file, snaking to the river. They have tied weights to the knots of their ankles. One step. Two step. One-by-one. I watch them the way a morning person hears the birds.

If you keep walking, you could go all the way to your end. But walking is also a kind of birth.

Considering the intensity of the way we enter into the world, pushed out, squeezed around our skin, it's no wonder we crave such massive feeling. War strategies. Highs so high. Sorrow about someone else's sorrow. Neither the girls nor the drunks have eaten in three days.

It is hunger or worry that keeps me twist-tied to the town, though sometimes I say it is love. I enter the diner when I mean to just keep walking. I have five dollars. A quiet appetite. A bright gray vision. I have just so many days and so many eyes. I will eat, circle, hunger, eat, the way I will go on loving anything I do not fear.

ARMIES

All the tiniest girls in the world live here. I notice them, sometimes, as they crawl through the old gray cracks between the wooden floorboards. I notice them from my bed when I am lying there, too tired to pick up any devices, too tired even to wait.

But usually I am waiting. Waiting at the kitchen table for the coffee pot to fill. Waiting for my husband's head and mine to merge like I know they are supposed to. Waiting until I change my mind, or don't. Waiting until I am finally old.

The tiny girls, all the while, are marching to and fro, on some kind of mission assigned by some kind of angel, or devil, or ancient genetic code. They are moving by instinct, that old pulse some men don't take seriously.

They march, I imagine, in kaleidoscopic ways. Zoom in, and their movements make the same patterns as the cells in their bodies, the same repeating shapes. Zoom all the way out, to outer space, and the stars are making the same patterns, too.

My lover is doing the dishes. I am near him at the kitchen table, waiting for the coffee. I am feeling the girls' tiny bodies patter beneath my hand, as though my hand were a small, protective roof. I wait so long that I question my waiting. I wait so long that I become angry. I wait so long that I question the validity of my anger. My lover drops a dish, and I flinch. I flatten the roof to the ground.

I TOO AM ONLY DREAMING

We only have one bedroom in our house and only one painting in our bedroom. It's the only painting in the whole house too. Our house is the only one built on a very quiet country road in Africa. The name of the county is Africa—the only one in the entire United States.

Although I understand that I am here, and not across the globe in Africa, there is something powerful in a proper noun, the way it pocks two things the same. I'm lonely, though I feel a private bond with strangers across the globe. When I lie awake in bed late at night, my head sometimes swarms with daytime Africans, eating, sleeping, making do.

Sometimes, should I say often, I cannot sleep at night. My brain's bed falls apart. Acute insomnia is difficult to explain. People ask, "Doesn't it drive you crazy?" I tell them that it used to. Now, I am used to insomnia and insomnia is used to me.

When I cannot sleep at night, I am unable to do anything productive. The this-and-that that fills our days when living. The chores on my clean-the-house list. There are seven chores on the list and, if I were capable, I would begin with number seven and work my way to one. For me, diminishment has always felt more like progress than accumulation has.

Number seven is organizing my shoebox of shoelaces. What a tangled mess, that box, packed and knotted and spilling from the brim. I shudder just to think. I cannot perform number seven while all the people here have embarked on private journeys through their own dream worlds. I am untangling the fibers of a scrambled mesh of thought, attempting to organize the cause-and-effect of history, which has forced me to be so—so! I too, am only dreaming, reaching to calm my homeless mind. I would like to tether sleep to me.

Sometimes, I try to think of insomnia as its own dream world. This is facilitated by staring at the painting on the bedroom wall. It is a painting of a girl strumming a tear-shaped instrument. The painter worked minimally, with fine strokes and lots of white space between. Only slight, dim swooshes make the girl's curving back, her long slender arms and longer, slenderer fingers. Her proportions are a bit bizarre.

When I look at this painting, my head propped on

two pillows, I like to imagine sitting there inside that canvas whiteness, listening to the most silent song in the world. I find a shady apple tree to lie down under and the girl plays and stays and plays. It is all she can do, the instrument painted to her lap, her seat painted to the soil, and I would like to listen always to that most beautiful silent sound, but what risk!

If I stay too long, I will become the soil, get sucked up by the apple tree's thick roots, become an apple myself. Instead, I stand and leave the silence. From afar, I count apples much like an insomniac counts sheep. I count the apples until they look like girls and taste like sheep. Until my husband, sleeping next to me, begins to snore like a bore stuck in a storm, catching raindrops with its snout. Then, the apples disappear and I am hungry.

One night, while I had been lying awake, my dear friend Marie phoned. She pardoned herself for calling so late, but was herself unable to sleep, and wanted somebody to talk to. Good thing I was awake. She had been studying lakes in Africa. She told me story about a breed of zooplankton called Daphnia pulicaria, who are all female and reproduce asexually in favorable conditions. They clone the unborn into being: no genetic diversity whatsoever. When environmental conditions deteriorate, pulicaria produce special male mates. The males for mating save the race. Marie is just wild about zooplankton.

When she had tired herself out, she thanked me for listening, and we said goodnight. I imagined a strange illness, much like insomnia, though instead of an inability to sleep there is an inability to be male and also to stay singular. When I tell people I do not sleep at night, I tell them things could be worse.

I could be the homeless man, or woman (I cannot tell, it is dark), who pees late-night in our backyard, after my husband has found his sleep. S/he steadies the body with one hand on the fence and bends forward, crouching, relieving all that liquid waste. Then the homeless person moves away from the fence very slowly as though s/he has no county, no continent, no legs.

I have never told my husband about the woman or man who pees. He would get angry and go on about the dangers of strangers. My husband owns a shotgun and does not trust trespassers. What if s/he was a druggie, pillaging for a fix? What if s/he was a rapist, thief, or worse? His speculations feel wrong, but he could be right. Who knows?

I would not tell my husband of the homeless visitor, as I could never discuss my wildest dreams. In one wildest dream, s/he is a messenger sent from God, who asks me to imagine us all in the afterlife, not winged and golden but completely nurtured and nurturing, like oneness. I sometimes nap in daytime, when there's light.

The girl in the painting is drawn so minimally, she may very well be a boy. She has no womanly curves and only long hair to suggest she's a girl. My husband told me once that he is attracted to women with very short hair. During his college years, he had approached such a woman in a crowded bar. When he offered to buy her a drink she smiled at him sweetly and told him she was gay.

"Oh, sorry," he said, blushing, moving away.

"A girl with short hair shows she isn't owned by social convention," he had told me.

The longest and slenderest part of the body is the small intestines. I wonder how the artist, if inclined, might choose to paint the strumming girl's small intestines. Long and slender like her arms? Longer and slenderer like her fingers? Would he paint them so long and slender that if the girl was murdered by a stranger with a shotgun we could make infinite guitar stings out of the coil? Would I lace her fibers through my shoes and wander? Would I tie a noose for me, or cook the meat into my husband's dinner food? In life as in dreams, light turns to shadow so quickly. One cannot see a difference if one tries.

"Did you ever think to grow your hair long instead of dating girls with short hair?" I asked my husband.

"Never," he said. It was night, and soon he fell

asleep. He woke at 11:15, 11:39, 12:07, 1:09, 1:56, 2:45, 4:18, 4:21, 5:11, and 6:45. He fell back asleep these very same moments.

Unslept for days, I begin to think I could be African, or bald, or something painted up. Unsplept for weeks, I begin to feel as though I were no one at all, limbs shrinking in, body expanding—amorphous blob. Unslept, I think of the way we start, singled-celled and total. Then dividing, multiplying, we become our selves, and we are each ourselves, all together.

I exhaust myself for days and days until I cannot hold a thread of thought. I exhaust myself until, surrender! Sleep creeps up, singing lullabies.

You are definite and imprecise, still and always moving, you are here always and never. You are good and bad, it's true. I sleep, then. It is all I need. I will sleep and sleep until hunger wakes me. One must also eat.

THE DAY THERE WAS A PICNIC

At the corner store, patrons were making love trans- actions, swapping money for the largest quantities of affection they can hurl over their shoulders and haul away. I didn't have any money, and love, who knows? But the people looked so happy. Or else sad. I couldn't tell.

It was so windy outside we could hardly stand. We pressed our bodies into an invisible wall. Then the rain came. Then the snow. Then displaced objects began to fall from the sky. Telephone booths and abacuses, dryer sheets and prisoners of war.

We covered our faces with our arms, hoped for the best—for life to continue, for whatever we already had. We stood blinded that way, until all the mad weather simply stopped.

Thankful, we set picnic tables and red checkered blankets out on the road in front of the corner store. We forced the cars to honk and go around. We ate up all the love that had been bought, then stuffed on the feast, waddled back to our own homes.

I didn't sleep well that night. My body ached in ways I never knew it could. I couldn't settle down, so I turned on a lamp. The light filled every corner of the room. It had a strange expansive quality, as though it would just keep going if I took a sledgehammer to the walls. To calm myself, I tried a form of meditation—with each inhale, I imagined sucking in a puff of clean white air. With each exhale I expelled thick black clouds of dust. Let the good in. Let the bad out. Let the good in.

I couldn't sustain the rhythm very long. Who was I to hoard all the earthly good, to send my black pain off like a forgotten daughter. I closed my eyes and felt a certain sense of hopelessness, thankful for the walls, for my own tiny world of love.

IPSEITY EPISTOLARY

Dear R,

Sitting by the sea at a dockside restaurant, in a new country, a colossal Jesus statue across the bay, you realize that your insides are not contained within you at all. Instead they surround you like your mother's once had. The sky is your durable, protective skin. The ocean is your brackish blood. The air, your lungs. The food you eat tastes of fish and spice, but you are only biting into your own glands and nodes, swollen a little in fever.

When did this begin? Your body, past its prime, contracts around the joints.

Once, your people thought the sun was a breed of god, but you knew better, you told them so. The sun is only something you coughed up. Your lover caught it in a tissue, tossed it askance.

No stray dogs skulk here. No wandering cows. Surely, there is life in the water, but when you look down you see only a floating cigarette butt, and piece of severed seaweed nudging its way to a fissured shore that needs some stitching up.

Love, R

Dear R,

Something is falling amidst the rain. A blue-green sadness that tastes of chalk. Who still cares to consider the sky swelling up, ready to overflow itself?

At some point in my life, I contained infinite bodies, lovely as seashells each, coiled and clamped around a living thing.

In my new apartment, rain sounds like the silence I left in my childhood bed, where I buried myself in night-light glow. Over the years, I've left silence in so many places, so many wrong turns that ended this way.

Yesterday, I made wrong turns driving to the county fair, but found my way eventually. The rabble there kept its distance and frowned. Bearded ladies and tattooed strongmen. Desperate clowns and vendors hawking candy-colored popcorn. They were all in cahoots against me. Perhaps they did not understand the freak of my unspeaking.

As I lifted to the top of the Ferris wheel, the carnival music warped and turned menacing. It was not the music, but my ears that contained the possibility of danger. My ears and my eyes, which, so high and alone, could map all the wrong turns I made driving myself here.

Love, R

Dear R,

Accidentally, I shined the lamp light into the cat's face. It was a minor act careless violence. I only wanted to fathom him better, know what he would do. He squawked a quick, disturbing sound, an almost-human intonation, and I suddenly understood why someone might say the path to the universal is through the individual.

It wouldn't be the first time I scared something off. Half of me is always scaring away the other half. My body and my mind. My limbs and my torso. It's like that bullfight I saw in Mexico once. Rodeo clowns pulled two fools from the audience, plopped each onto a side of a seesaw, then released the bull. One frightened person sprung into the air while the other was pushed to the dirt. I'd seen this before, I think I've lived it.

I keep thinking something is about to change. I don't know exactly what, but it's immense. Maybe they'll have to evacuate California because the earthquakes, the big ones, will finally arrive. Maybe they'll colonize Mars, and I'll go too. I'd like to be one of the first to drag my foot through all that red, to look down over the quiet earth and understand the smallness of my absence.

Maybe someone will listen when I say, it was always going to end like this, and so it's already ended. It's only human loneliness we are feeling, after all. It's only the kind of betrayal that's bound to itself and desires nothing.

Love, R

Dear R,

I poured myself a glass of wine in the middle of the afternoon. My body and my mind hurt so bad, I thought fuck it. Then I watched an inspirational video where a woman told me to never dim my light. She was very persuasive. She had a voice like a siren. She said, "Turn it up, shine your light," like a lunatic or a saint.

I have to say, she made me feel better. She made me feel like I could do anything. Throw myself off a six-story building and survive. That's the funny thing about feelings. They're so fickle they almost mean nothing.

I'm living in a valley between two mountains, thinking about all the wild weather that occurs. But snowstorms and lightning aren't what really stand the test of time. Not even these two mountains will make it, in the end. Someday you won't look at me the same.

I can hide almost everything about myself, but the

aging of my body can't lie. There's always Botox, I suppose. I could try to be a statue made of stone.

Do you think it would be nice if I visited you soon? Leave the echoes of this valley, meet you at your seaside dock?

Let's try this: We crumble together. I'll hold your best pieces in the palms of my hands, and you can hold my hands when they fall off. I'll be surrounded by all that you contain. You can throw my map of wrong turns deep into the sea.

Love, R

WHAT WE BURY

Sometimes the birds are floating in an imperfect V, the birches bloom, and beyond them, blue. The sun threads gold into the waving sheets on the laundry line. In this moment, there is so much beauty in the world that death must also be beautiful. This is when I love so much I can't believe it. This is when I love so much I can't breathe.

My grandfather stopped breathing a year before he died. We sat in a park, held hands. He ripped out a page of his sketchbook, gave it to me. We drew one of the strange imported trees they put in the center of all the landscaping, the kind of tangled tree that looks like it's strangling itself. After working a while, I looked down at my grandfather's page. I had expected to find a masterpiece. I was told he had been a brilliant artist, or wanted to be, or should have been. I was disappointed with the sparse, light lines on his page, because I didn't understand beginnings.

I was afraid of death and I knew my grandfather was

very old. I told myself I had better make sure he knows I love him. The sun had stopped refracting shades of gold the year I told him "I love you" a million times.

Before he died, he hollowed out a space for me in his chest that I could fit into if I crouched. But I had already done for him all I could.

We buried other things inside him instead. A flower petal pawed free by a long-haired cat. Paint painted over wallpaper. A covered bridge over a dried-up river. Slippers that make feet sweat. A third-floor fire escape, with rust. Two girls riding bikes, one popping a wheelie. A brass wrist cuff and a tiger's-eye ring. Drawing paper and a charcoal stick. A shovel scraping ice. An unfolded blanket left on a beige couch. A knot in a plank of the scuffed wood floor. A pair of world wars. A fully occupied strip of power outlets. Power outlets plugged into power outlets late at night. A night light. A hammer left under the porch. A child's bathrobe. A bee's torso on a window sill. A pair of antique mirrors that reflect each other just as far as space and time.

THREE WOMEN I ALMOST LOVED

One.

She said: In my home, I want to feel at home. I want to feel as though I am swaddled in a blanket, as though the walls pump food right to my gut. I water the plants, all seven or eight, some dying. I feed the cat. I want the air to be humid because moisture is life. How many bugs live here? How many living organisms? What don't I see? You know, I once was capable of so much love. Come in. In my home, I want to have everybody over for a their favorite drinks and talk all night with music playing. Come in. I say it not like I'm begging you. I don't want to recall anymore. I'm done with recalling. I could spend one year painting the same painting, blending all the faults. I could move to a fault line and play this game I'm already playing: anything could happen at any time, assuming time is, you know, real. I watch ten children get sucked into a fault line, no? I watch one moon implode. Here, I'm confusing what happens with what might. What can with what can in my head. I watch a set of angels play make believe. Are you getting this? Are you seeing this too? Two angels now are breathing under water. Now their parents never aged. Now, and only now, their home is lit up like a dry Christmas tree, nothing but good warmth. I once told a man all I wanted was to be warm. He said he knew it. I want, in my home, to rip my face off, smatter it across the ceiling and say, "Now I don't have a face. I am happy." Look into your ribcage... are you all there? Where does your home end and end? Look, I'm speaking into this one side, trying to reach the other, then I'm not even sure there are two sides. Have you opened your windows lately? Have you cleaned the dust and dead house flies from the sill, and the bee? Have you heard the neighbors, the new ones, not the addict who moved out? No cops anymore, no pleading apologies. I'm not about you, but if you come over, I'll open the windows for you. I'll give you a seat. I'll set the breeze to your skin. I'll be quiet about, well everything. I'll let you close the window if you get cold. I'll douse my rocking chair and bury my dead horse.

Two.

1. I never met my mother.
2. She died as they cut me out of her.
3. She was thirty-five years younger than my father.

4. She had brown hair like me, but blue eyes, which are the rarest. The allele always recessive.

5. In her diary, she wrote that her great-grandfather fled Sicily for America on the RMS Carpathia. He was just a boy and escaping death in the hands of La Cosa Nostra, with twelve dollars sewn into the lining of his jacket.

6. I keep her diary in my sock drawer, next to my condoms and spare change.

7. Once, I thought I saw my mother's ghost washing the dishes in the kitchen sink while my father and I watched a Dodgers game.

8. My father said my mother had not been right in the head. He said she was loud and nagging and lazy. He said, had she lived, their relationship would not have.

9. In her diary, she drew little pictures of what she saw: small birds, a lost mitten, a pencil, a lamp.

10. When I have a child, I will cut nothing out. I will sew all our ghosts into the lining of our pockets.

Three.

I know this doesn't sound good, but I promise it's not so terrible. I used to be really sick, near death. Without going into detail: It was as much my own fault as it was my genetics. It was as much genetics as it was the people in my life not being able to overcome their fear, not helping me during my time of need. I don't hold it against them now, but most people have no idea how to deal with other people's pain.

I was getting to rock bottom. It was like Hemingway wrote about bankruptcy: It happens gradually, then suddenly. On the way to the bottom, I vomited in the bathroom at work on a regular basis. My car was a fucking mess. Sticky, sometimes bloody tissues scatterer about. Bottles and wrappers. Stains and smears. Then I caught pneumonia, passed out, hit my temple on the corner of the dresser going down. When it was happening, slowly, then the suddenly, I hid in my room, away from my roommates. I kept my grades up in my classes, because I thought, if I manage do one thing well, maybe I can fool the world. I forgot to take showers. I cheated on my long-distance girlfriend with a stranger, because I knew the truth: She could never love someone like the real me. Some people with my problems actually die. I've known a couple of them personally. I consider myself lucky that I just visited underworld for a time, hit the bottom and crawled back out.

I went up to New Hampshire for a winter. Only eleven miles of coastline but it's beautifully cold and sharp and mostly empty. No matter how many layers of coats and long Johns I wore, no matter how warm my hat, the wind cut through. The lobster shacks were boarded up and the bandstand stayed empty. The waves crashed and crashed over rocks, and seaweed froze brittle with frost. The funny thing about needing time to yourself, about needing to be in a place to be fetal and naked: You never really are alone. The surfers came out no matter what. So did the squawking seagulls pecking at loose shells. So did the stars.

This one night I stripped down and ran naked across the snow-covered beach. I dove straight into the icy salt water. I stayed there, waiting for the cold to kick in, to feel again. I shivered and stared out across the sea that was heavy and black and did not end until Europe. Then I turned back to look at the beach. There was a woman. Her hair looked matted and dreadlocked. Her formless sort of body was covered in rags. In her hand she swayed a metal detector like a metronome...back forth...back forth...back forth...back forth. I felt my heart swell, there's no other way to say it, and it kept swelling until I needed to move and almost couldn't breath. I remembered, then, that this was the feeling that had me reeling towards the underworld, towards rock bottom, in the first place. I guess I am a liar, and it *is* so terrible. Too much love, and no place to put it. Too much love that it can't be anything but wasted. Too much love in a world like this.

ACKNOWLEDGMENTS

Many thanks to Alban Fischer, Madeleine Maillet, Katie Anderson, Nina Puro, John Colasacco, Bailey Seybolt, Taylor Collier, Mildred Barya, David Nutt, Stuart Ross, Annie Liontas, Emily Schultz, the Syracuse University MFA class of 2012, Amisha Patel, Jess von Sück, Rivka Galchen, Lisa Romagnoli, and Michael Czyzniejewski. I'm grateful to my teachers and mentors, Arthur Flowers, George Saunders, Dana Spiotta, Michael Burkard, Bob Gates, and Mikhail Iossel. Thanks to publishers and editors of earlier versions of these stories, and to the places and organizations that generously supported me, including Syracuse University, the Disquiet International Literary Program, and the Barbara Ingram School for the Arts Foundation. To Tina, Alan, and Samantha Fishow, I'm grateful for your inspiration and encouragement. Thanks for being my family. Finally, I could not have written this book without my husband, Daniel. Thank you and I love you.

PUBLICATION CREDITS

Some of the stories in this book have appeared in earlier forms in the following publications: *Connotation Press*, *Cosmonauts Avenue*, *The Fiddleback*, *Hobart*, *Jellyfish Review*, *Joyland*, *Juked*, *Masque and Spectacle*, *Matrix Magazine*, *Monkeybicycle*, *Mud Season Review*, *Necessary Fiction*, *Oblong*, *Quarterly West*, *Requited*, *Room*, *Smokelong Quarterly*, *Tin House*, *The Tishman Review*, and *Vestal Review*. A selection of stories in this book also appeared in the chapbook *The Opposite of Entropy*, published by Proper Tales Press.